I0452776

The Zion Trail

Also by Marsha Ward

The Owen Family Saga

Gone for a Soldier
The Man from Shenandoah
Ride to Raton
Trail of Storms
Spinster's Folly

The Zion Trail

A Promised Valley Novel

Marsha Ward

WestWard Books
꙳◆꙳
Payson, Arizona

The Zion Trail
Copyright © 2016 Marsha Ward

Cover Design by Linda Boulanger
www.telltalebookcovers.weebly.com

All rights reserved.

No part of this book may be reproduced in any form or by
any means without prior written permission of the publisher,
except in the case of brief passages embodied in reviews and
articles.

This is a work of fiction. The characters, places, and incidents
are either the product of the author's imagination or are
represented fictitiously. Most settings and events of the early
Mormon Church era, as well as some speeches and
declarations made by the historical figures as depicted herein
are recorded in historical documents and records. The author
has made every possible effort to portray them accurately. A
few pieces of dialogue—such as ordinary conversations—are
imaginary and fictitious.

Published by WestWard Books
P. O. Box 53
Payson, Arizona

E-book edition released February 2016
Paperback edition released March 2016
ISBN 13: 978-0-9883810-8-7

Dedication

To Joseph Smith, the Prophet of the Restoration.

Acknowledgements

I owe a tremendous debt of gratitude to my wonderful Beta Readers, Patricia Nipper, Kari Pike, Becky Rohner, and Deb Eaton. Without their time, efforts, and suggestions, this novel would not have been published. Thanks to P. J. Switzer, Amber Hall, and members of my ANWA Chapter, Moonwriting, who read and critiqued key scenes and chapters. Thanks to Jae Hall and her husband, for their help on the manner of crafting Prairie Diamonds (horseshoe nail rings). Especial thanks to Laura Byrd for allowing me to use names of her pioneer ancestors for a few of my characters, and to her, Lynn Gardner, and Joy Dawn Johnson for their donations to author Rachel Ann Nunes' fight against plagiarism.

I also owe thanks to my pioneer ancestors, from some of whom I borrowed names for my characters.

Chapter 1

After I made a half-circle turn at the end of the row of corn, I pulled Tom, our plow horse, to a halt, swept off my old hat, and wiped the trickles of sweat from my eyes with the back of my wrist. Then I ran my fingers through my dripping hair to train it back from my eyes, for whatever good that would do. August had been plenty hot this year of Our Lord, eighteen forty-three. The cool breezes of autumn couldn't come fast enough to suit me.

Settling my hat once again on my head, I ran a glance over the field, checking my work. In the tail of my eye I caught movement on the road from the west.

I turned to look directly at the road. Across the rows of young corn stalks, I saw dust rising slowly into the air as two figures walked along the dry surface of the lane. By their dress, I knew them for strangers, for no one in our part of Pennsylvania wore a black suit except on Sunday, and this was Tuesday.

Curiosity being part of my makeup, I leaned on a plow handle for a while, watching their progress and wondering about their errand. By and by they saw me. When they came alongside my position, they hopped the ditch to approach the fence.

At fifteen years of age, I had reached nearly my full growth, and I wasn't beyond considering myself a man. I did as much on the farm as my father did, except for the planning and the worrying, so I wasn't surprised when they hailed me as a man.

"Hello, Brother," the taller of the two men called. "Can you give us a drink?" He indicated my water bucket sitting under a tree near the fence.

I wrapped the lines around the plow handles, strode over to retrieve the bucket, and carried it to the fence.

"Plenty, and welcome," I said, giving my father's standard reply. I shooed away a drinking yellow jacket and lifted the pail to the top of the fence.

The man who had addressed me drank first. I guessed that he was older by three or four years than the shorter man. As they slaked their thirst, I wondered how long since they had tasted water, for they drank with great gusto and an air of thankfulness.

Their suits were covered with the fine dust that abounded on our roads, but they seemed not to mind, giving all their thoughts to dipping water from the pail and letting it slide down their dusty throats.

While the younger man drank, the older one looked at me and smiled. "We're grateful for the water," he said. "Thank you, young man. It's been a long, dusty walk."

I nodded to acknowledge his thanks. "You're welcome to all you can drink." I stuck out my hand and pumped the one he offered. "My name is Elijah Marshall."

"I'm Nathan Caldwell," he said, letting go of my hand. "My companion is Matthew Long. We're ministers of the gospel, come to your neighborhood looking for an opportunity to preach."

"Pa will be glad to see you. He's a God-fearing man, a seeker after truth. Men of the Lord are welcome in his house." I squinted up at the sun. "It's nearly dinner time. Come and eat with us."

Mr. Long grinned his acceptance. "Much obliged," he said.

"Just follow the road to the first lane on the right," I directed them. "Tell my mother that Lije sent you. I'll be along with the horse by and by."

They waved their thanks and jumped the ditch back to the road. I hauled the bucket off the fence and turned back to the plow. Old Tom still stood where I'd reined him in, flicking flies away with his tail and standing three-legged in the heat of the sun. His ears twitched at my approach, and I patted his flank before I unhitched him from the plow.

"Tom, boy, we've got company. Won't that make Ma's eyes dance!"

~ ~ ~ ~ ~

Old Tom turned to regard me for a moment, then faced front again before he shook his head to rid himself of the persistent flies.

I kept a hold on the empty bucket as I shinnied up onto Tom's broad brown back. The harness had soaked up the rays of the morning sun, and I could feel the warmth of it beneath my legs. With a touch of my bare heels into Tom's ribs, I started him for the gate at the edge of the field.

I wished that Tom was a jumper, but he was too old and stout for that activity, so I got down from his back to open the gate and let him through. After closing the gate behind us to keep the cows out of the corn, I climbed again to my perch and urged the horse forward.

Before long, as we moved into the shade of the trees planted on both sides of the back lane, I smelled dinner cooking. The trees had invited a breeze to enjoy the shade, and Tom and I relished the cool air and savory odors that flowed through the green tunnel.

As I slid off Tom in the barnyard, I saw the two ministers walking up the lane toward our house. I gave them a wave, and then led Tom into the barn.

When I returned from tending the horse, I didn't see the men outside, and hoped that my mother had already bade the visitors welcome. I went to the back of the house, beat the dust from my overalls, and scrubbed the grime of the morning's work from my arms and face. Then I combed my hair into a degree of tidiness.

My hair was thick and dark like my father's but more often than not, it refused to take orders from my hand and fell forward into my eyes. I gave it one more pass with the comb, then opened the door to the kitchen and hung my hat on a nail.

"Here, Lije. Take this."

My mother shoved a bowl of sausages into my hands and pointed me to the doorway. "Since you're going that way, you may as well put that on the table." She laughed as I furrowed my brows in chagrin. "Go along, now. No one's going to think less of you if you set food on the table."

I brushed aside my worries on that score and instead, inhaled deeply and filled my lungs with the sweet, piquant odor of home-made sausage links. Ma loved to cook and did ample justice to the task. I elbowed open the connecting door and made my way to the table.

I caught my sister Sarah smiling at the two young ministers as she set plates around the table. Sarah carried two more years than me and fancied herself to be quite a grownup young lady. I put the bowl on the table and got out of her way before she smacked me with the back of a spoon. Then I remembered that with visitors present, she would likely be on her best behavior.

The hair I had so neatly combed just minutes before sprang forward to fall across my brow, and I gave my head a sideways shake as I walked over to talk with our guests. The shake didn't serve. I had to resort to a quick thrust of my fingers to control the unruly shock of hair.

Mr. Long grinned at me, gesturing toward my head. "It disconveniences a man," he said.

I grinned back, completely won over by his candor.

Just as I was about to sit on a low stool at his feet, my father came into the room, and I jumped up to make him acquainted with our visitors.

"Pa, these men are ministers of God," I said. "I invited them to take dinner with us."

The preachers were on their feet, and my father moved over to shake their hands.

"This is Nathan Caldwell," I said with a nod, "and Matthew Long. My father, James Marshall. Pa, they've come to share the Word hereabouts."

"We appreciate your son's invitation to eat," Mr. Caldwell said as he shook Pa's hand. "I thank you for raising a mannerly boy."

The word "boy" cut into my feelings for a time, but not deeply enough to keep me from hearing Pa's reply.

"That's our way. I'd take it strange of him if he'd let you pass by." Pa motioned the preachers back into their seats. "My wife will have the meal on directly." He took his chair and leaned forward. "What message have you brought us?"

My chance to speak alone to the men had disappeared with my father's appearance, so I went over to Sarah and politely asked her if she needed help with anything. She looked at me as though I had taken leave of my brains, and I grinned at her. I, too, was on my toes with guests in the house.

Sarah didn't offer to share the work with me, so I wandered into the kitchen to see what I could do to hurry dinner.

"Oh good, Lije. Take that kettle off the hook and bring it here to the table. It's too full for me to lift, and your pa's gone in to talk with the preachers."

I unhooked the kettle, and grunting a little at its weight, carried it to the work table. It was plenty heavy, and I was glad I'd come along to help. Pa had raised me up to be helpful to women folk. Although Ma was strong, I had a notion she shouldn't be lifting heavy iron kettles around. Under the front of her apron, she sported a slight swelling. I figured that in due time there'd be another little Marshall sitting up to table.

"What else, Ma?"

She reached up to smooth back my front hair.

"As soon as I dish up this stew, you can take the tureen to the table. I expect your pa and those ministers will have taken each other's measure by now."

"Where's John?" I looked out the window for my younger brother.

"I sent him to Mrs. Tisdale's on an errand. He'll be back by and by." She paused and appeared to be thinking, as her brow furrowed like it always did when she took time to contemplate. "Never mind carrying in the stew. I'll get Sarah to do that. You go fetch Mary Eliza. She's out in the barn fussing over those kittens."

"I hope she's staying clear of the horses."

"I warned her again. Go bring her in, won't you, Lije?"

"Sure, Ma."

She lifted the lid on the kettle, and I took a sniff of the savory odors that filled the room before I opened the door. Eager to return to enjoy the promised feast, I hurried across the yard.

The bottom half of the two-piece door to the barn's tack room stood open. I ducked under the top half and entered. Our barn cat, Calico, had—since the birth of her latest litter of kittens—taken up residence in a wooden box at the rear of the room. As my eyes adjusted to the diminished light, I could see that Mary Eliza was not in the place.

I glanced into the box, noting that the mother was off on some adventure, leaving her young ones asleep. Likely my sister had followed the cat, eager to join in the fun.

I unlatched the top before I stepped through the doorway. As I went up the middle aisle, deeper into the barn,

I looked into each stall, expecting to find Mary Eliza trying to milk a cow or groom a horse. But she wasn't where I could catch a sight of her, and I was beginning to feel some worried.

Calico darted past my legs, startling me into backing up a step. She streaked back the way I had come, carrying a mouse in her mouth. I began to follow her, then stopped, feeling a fool, for the cat could tell me nothing.

"Mary Eliza, Ma wants you," I called into the vastness of the barn. My voice echoed a bit, then I heard my name whispered. The sound came from above me. I went toward the ladder that led upward and into the loft, fear blending with anger. Mary Eliza was forbidden to climb the ladder, for she was only three years old, and the height was dangerous if she fell.

I started up the ladder. When my head came level with the loft floor, I saw my sister a foot away, arms clasped around a beam, hugging it for all she was worth.

The sight of my plump sister clutching the beam cleansed the anger and the fear in my heart. In the midst of the instantaneous wash of relief, I asked, "Pumpkin, what are you doing? It's time for dinner. Come over here and Lije will give you a horsey ride."

"Lije, I scared." Her voice shook so that I hardly recognized it. "I scared," she repeated, remaining frozen to the beam.

"Here, now," I said, climbing slowly up the rest of the ladder. "Lije will come up and get you out of this dusty old loft."

I put out my hand to lift myself over the lip of the loft, and she closed her eyes and screamed.

I stopped, puzzled at her terror. Then I glanced over my shoulder and realized that from her position, she could see down to the floor of the barn, and it was a long distance.

She finished her scream, sniffled twice, and whispered,

"I fall, Lije." Then she hiccoughed.

If I climbed up one more rung I could reach my sister without too much trouble, but if she fought me, we could both tumble off the ladder. I had to calm her first.

"Did you get to play with the kittens, Pumpkin?" I asked, watching to see if my words distracted her from staring over the lip of the loft.

She paid me no mind, so I tried again.

"I saw Calico run past with a mouse for dinner," I ventured. This time her eyes lifted from the floor and met mine. I moved as swiftly as I dared, prying her chubby hands from around the beam with one of mine as I held to the ladder with the other.

"Come on," I pleaded with her, half to myself. "Let loose."

She came to me with a rush, and I was hard-pressed to hold her as we swayed at the top of the ladder. I thanked the Lord it was firmly spiked to the edge of the loft.

She sobbed against me as I sidestepped my way down the ladder, breathing a little raggedly myself. At the bottom I resisted a powerful urge to let my tongue thrash her ears, but she was only three, and I was so glad we were safe that I hugged her instead.

I boosted her up onto my shoulders and carried her to the back door, then put her down and dusted her off. Cobwebs clung to her hair, but despite her struggles, I got most of them combed out, and washed her face and hands until she looked presentable. Then I took her to Ma.

"She was up in the loft, grabbing a beam. There's some splinters in her hands, but at least they're clean."

"Thank you, son." Ma picked up the last dish of food. "Don't you go up that ladder alone, Mary Eliza," she declared, then went into the parlor.

I followed and stood Mary Eliza at her place at table, then took mine. Pa brought the ministers over, still talking, and indicated seats of honor for them, but no one sat, for Pa stood behind his chair, and the ministers followed our example.

"We'll say grace before we partake," Pa informed them, then bowed his head and launched into a long recitation of thanksgiving.

My place was near to the pot of stew, which filled the air with the odors of savory and thyme, mixed with onion and parsnip. My mouth watered as I listened to the prayer, and I admit that at least half my mind was on a fast filling of my stomach, and not upon returning thanks for the food before me.

Pa ended with a firm "Amen," and the preachers added their voices to the chorus, then we sat, and Pa dished up the stew into the stack of bowls beside him.

From that time on, I devoted my attention to my food. I had put in a long morning's work, and I had a hollow leg to fill.

On the fringes of my consciousness, I heard my father tell my mother about the religion that the ministers preached.

"They've come to bring members to the Church of Jesus Christ of Latter-day Saints, Emily." I'd never heard of that church, and wasn't much interested, so I kept shoveling my food into my mouth as politely as a hungry fifteen-year-old could do.

Pa spoke more, about a prophet named Joseph Smith, and him restoring Christ's church. Then he said, "They're sent here by Jesus Christ," and I about dropped my fork on the floor as the hairs on the back of my neck rose.

These men claimed to represent The Lord himself, and that got my attention. I counted that a weighty thing, and held my breath waiting for my father's next words.

"We'll hear them out following dinner," he said.

I let out the breath I was holding and grabbed another. Pa was going to give up an afternoon's work to listen to two strangers.

~ ~ ~ ~ ~

After supper that evening, the "elders," as the ministers asked us to call them, continued to explain their beliefs, and told of the place from which they had come, a city they called "Nauvoo." They considered it to be "Zion," a special dwelling place where lived the pure in heart. The way they spoke of it, Zion must be heaven on earth.

They also mentioned more about the Prophet Joseph, telling us about his brother Hyrum, with whom he shared a close bond, and other members of the Smith family. They had believed and supported Joseph in his holy work.

I looked at my brother John. If he said he had seen God and Jesus Christ, would I believe him? I would have to give that idea more thought.

Pa seemed to take no notice that we had spent a half day listening to the things they had to say. He was so engrossed by their teaching that he missed it entirely when Sarah slipped out, "to wash up the dishes," she said, but I didn't hear any noises from the kitchen except the quiet closing of the back door.

Soon after that, I excused myself to take care of the chores before night fell. Pa nodded absently when I asked leave to go, and I wondered what had taken hold of his wits. Everything the elders said made perfect sense to me, so I was amazed at his abstraction.

I was slopping our sow and her brood when I first became aware of the voices. The pigpen was built up next to the hen house, and Sarah must've come out to check for any late-laid eggs. But somebody had joined her in there, and from the words that wiggled through the cracks, that somebody's hands weren't gathering eggs.

Curious, I found a knot hole in the side of the coop, and took a sight around the interior.

Hans Stiles, a brawny young farmer from down the road a piece, had his arms around my sister, and she wasn't struggling any. In fact, from the look on her face, I figured she was mighty content. My heart lurched. Hans had bullied me several times through the years before I began to add inches to my height. I knew him to have a wicked temper. I thought my sister had more sense than to see *him* as a suitor.

"Then they started in telling Pa about their religion," she told Hans. "He's still sitting there, listening to every word they say."

"But they are not from around here?"

"They come from Illinois. Some place called Nauvoo."

"Ah, hell!" Hans dropped his hands from Sarah's shoulders. "It's those damned Mormons!"

"Mormons?" Sarah asked in a squeaky voice. "Are you certain? They didn't use that name."

"If they came from Nauvoo, they're Mormons, all right." Hans shook his finger in front of her nose. "Don't you have anything to do with them. They have ways you can't trust. They'll put a brand on you and sell you into slavery."

The light was kind of dim in the chicken coop, but I still saw my sister's body jump and shake with terror. "A . . . a brand? Are they devils?"

"Pretty near. They don't believe in Jesus. They worship Beelzebub, you know."

"Oh Hans! They're in our house. My pa is listening to them."

"Your old man always was soft on anyone who said he was a religionist. You stay away from them, hear? I'll take care of them. You stay clear of their preaching."

"What if Pa makes me listen?" she whispered.

"Don't let them lay claim on you. I heard about them. They take all the women folk they can gather up and ship them off to their city. Then nobody ever hears from them again." Oddly enough, he grinned. "I hear they make girls marry the leaders, the ones with the horns underneath their hats and the tails growing inside their trousers. And the worst thing is, the leaders are already married, sometimes to twenty-five other women."

I thought Sarah was going to faint, she was that white.

My ire flared, and I wanted to beat Hans Stiles into the ground. How dare he menace my sister with his evil words?

He seemed to be holding Sarah upright, and for a while, he kind of soothed her with soft words, which was strange, after he'd done all he could to scare her.

I was angry, not at the elders for trying to mislead my pa, but at Hans for frightening Sarah with his awful tales. I knew down in my belly they weren't true. From the feeling that I had when I listened to the elders, I could tell who was spouting lies.

My cramped position had inhibited the flow of blood to my arms, and I staggered away from the knothole so I could beat blood back into them. For a moment, I thought of telling Pa that Hans was leading Sarah down the primrose path, but wondered if he would take time away from listening to the elders to pay heed to my tale. By the time I could go get Pa, Hans might to be gone. Besides, if I interfered with her swain, Sarah would surely be my enemy, and she could slap and bite until the sun set.

When I returned to the peephole, Sarah and Hans were smooching, which gave me a sour stomach. No matter what I did, Sarah was already under Hans's influence, and I, her younger brother, would come off second best in any contest of wills.

I finally admitted I couldn't win and shrugged my shoulders, thinking that since she was seventeen, she was old enough now to make up her own mind. She was near to being a woman, and the day would come when she'd go off with a husband. From the things I'd seen and heard, I suspected that the day wasn't far off, no matter what I thought of Hans Stiles, so I quit spying on them and went back to my work.

Chapter 2

Because Pa asked the elders to stay the night, I knew he was seriously interested in their message. There were great gaps in my understanding of it all, but then, I wasn't hearing all the preaching. I was doing all the chores.

Pa had never acted like this before. It worried me. It wasn't like Pa to neglect his work.

The next morning I asked him at breakfast if I should continue with the cultivating that I had started yesterday. He nodded, absently, like a man far away. I looked at Ma, and she had a happy, glazed look on her face. I guessed then that our family was going to undergo a change in religious philosophy. That was all right with me. I liked the elders, especially Elder Long, and to my way of thinking, the things they told us were straight out and logical. I left the house and went about my work.

I enjoyed the morning in the cornfield. I was cultivating field corn, the part of the crop we left to mature to provide feed for our animals. The stalks stood way above my head, and though the work was dusty, it was shady. Old Tom pulled the plow slowly through the furrows while I made sure it was on a straight course between the cornstalks.

The earth was dry. We hadn't seen rain for a long while. Even though the plow moved slowly, it raised a cloud of fine dust that hovered around me, filling my nose with the smell of earth, my earth. Pa had given me this field, and I loved that odor, even when the dust caused me to sneeze. When time came for me to be on my own, this field would be the start for me and my family.

Of course, that was far in the future. I didn't have a girl. Indeed, I had no use for them. The farther I could keep myself away from girls, the better I liked it.

When the sun stood straight up in the sky, I left the plow in the field and rode Tom back to the barn. After putting him in his stall, rubbing him down, and giving him a bucket of water and a measure of oats, I washed up at the back of the house.

Ma was in the kitchen, putting slices of cold beef between slabs of bread.

"Is this for dinner, Ma?"

"Lije, it takes less time to prepare sandwiches than a meal. I don't want to miss any more of the elders' talk than I have to." She wiped her hands on her apron, and I again noticed the bulge on her front side. Ma caught me looking at her stomach, and she laughed. "Yes, I'm going to have a child, Lije. This one will grow up knowing the right way to live."

"What do you mean, Ma?" I suspected I knew the answer, but wanted confirmation.

"I'll let your pa say. You go in and listen to the elders. I fear you haven't heard enough of their preaching."

"There's been the work. Pa hasn't ever let the work go before."

She must have taken notice of my concern. "It'll be all right soon, Lije. Pa's been discussing religion with the elders all morning, and he's about learned all there is to know about their church." She smiled, a warm, secret smile that as much as told me what I wanted to know. "Now go in and take heed of the message."

I went.

~ ~ ~ ~ ~

Pa sat in his chair, reading from a book I'd never seen before. Elder Caldwell was directing him to find a particular passage. I slipped onto a stool, folding up my legs so I wouldn't have them in the way of anybody, and listened to my father's deep voice.

"Behold, I am Jesus Christ, whom the prophets testified shall come into the world. And behold, I am the light and the life of the world: and I have drunk out of that bitter cup which the Father hath given me."

The hair rose on my neck and arms. I didn't know the name of the book Pa was reading, but it surely was an extraordinary work, and whatever else it might be, the truth was in it.

Once the chill passed, and I was listening tight again, I found out from the discussion that Pa was reading a volume called the Book of Mormon. The elders said this was an ancient account of people who lived here in America long ago. Christ had visited those people, they said. My chest swelled with awe, and I paid close heed to the elders' words.

After Pa finished reading another passage, he looked up and addressed Elder Caldwell. "I'd like to purchase this book."

The elder gave him the price, and Pa rose right away and went to his room to fetch the money. He gave it to Elder Caldwell, who gave it to Elder Long. Pa picked up the book again and opened to the passage he had been reading. "This is a remarkable volume," he said, and both elders nodded and engaged themselves again in their teaching.

Sarah came in, somewhat hesitantly, I thought, and sat in the corner of the room, far from the "evil Mormons." My younger brother John brought in a smell of cow dung, breaking my concentration, and I wrinkled my nose at him. He got the message, left the room, and returned a few minutes later with scrubbed hands and face, scraped feet, and dusted overalls. I grinned at him. My ten-year-old brother smelled about the same, but he sure looked better.

Ma brought Mary Eliza into the room with her, and Pa broke off the conversation to approach the table.

As always, we stood around the table while Pa pronounced the blessing on the food. I noticed that his thanks was heavy for the arrival of the elders, more even than his thanks for the food.

When we sat down to our sandwiches and glasses of milk, Pa glanced around at the family.

"We've been greatly privileged by the visit of Elders Caldwell and Long. I have listened with great interest to their teachings. Their explanations of the Gospel are much different from that of Reverend Silcoe or any other preacher I've heard." He paused for a moment, clearing his throat. When he began again to speak, I saw a new light in his eyes.

"Their additional book of scripture has touched my soul," Pa said. "I believe what they have brought us is of great value. Your mother and I have discussed what we must do next." Again, he cleared his throat, gazing at Ma with such tenderness that I had to lower my eyes. "Tonight, we will unite ourselves to Christ's true church by baptism. All will be well."

Even as a warm feeling went through my body, I wondered what Reverend Silcoe, the minister of our church in town, would think of this turn of events.

I caught a low moan from Sarah's direction and turned to look at her. She sat at the corner of the table, not her usual place, but a spot far from the elders. Her face seemed rigid, probably frozen by her heed to Hans Stiles' lying stories. I imagined that cold fear was racing through her veins like water from a winter pond. I could tell she wasn't happy, but after that first sound, she didn't say another word.

Now I knew what Ma had meant in the kitchen. The babe she carried would learn a whole new religion at her knee, one that made perfect sense to me, from what I had heard of it.

Pa and Elder Caldwell went over the details of the

baptism. We were to gather on the banks of the mill pond after the sun went down.

"There might be opposition," the elder said.

Once we were all present, the elders would begin the service. Pa and Ma would be baptized first, then Sarah, me, and John. Mary Eliza, I learned, not yet eight years old, wasn't "accountable" and didn't need to be baptized tonight.

I wondered if Sarah was going to put up a fight. The way the elders explained it, they would actually touch us, putting us down into the pond water to wash away our sins, and I didn't think Sarah would allow that, not after what Hans had said.

I watched her for a while, and figured there was a struggle going on in her mind. Pa and Ma never even looked her way, so they didn't suspect her reaction to Pa's declaration.

Busy as she was looking inward, her eyes glazed over in her set face, Sarah didn't see my glances in her direction. I was sure she didn't know I had overheard Hans's warning. Fierce was her struggle, yet she never gathered the courage to say anything to Pa to contradict his plan.

Me, I was pleased at the prospect of joining a church that said Christ had visited this continent. The elders had told us of Joseph Smith, of how he prayed and was chosen to restore the correct church on the earth. I had a warm feeling for someone who had been called to be a prophet when he was not much younger than me. I suppose I borrowed much from the strength of Pa's testimony that day, but it was enough. I would enter the pond and undergo a dunking.

~ ~ ~ ~ ~

Pa surprised me by doing his own work that afternoon. I guess a peace came over him after his decision to have his family baptized, and his mind was freed to allow him to carry on with his life.

Notwithstanding his contentment, he took a plow into

the corn and cultivated a mighty big part of the fields. Old Bess must have stepped lively to cover all that ground.

Pa whistled around the barn that evening. Usually cheerful, my pa had been known to whistle before, but only on the happiest of occasions, so I knew our imminent baptism was giving him pleasure.

I didn't know how the elders kept busy without Pa to talk to, until that afternoon when I came upon a mended harness. The kindness saved me from doing the task, and I vowed to thank whichever elder had mended it for me.

After supper, the time approached for our baptism service, and Ma piled several quilts and blankets into my arms. I wondered why Pa didn't light a lantern, but once we stepped outside, I noticed the full moon had risen.

We walked the mile to the pond in silence. I think Sarah wanted to hang back, but I managed to get behind her to prevent that, reckoning that it would be a fine thing for all of our family members to have our sins washed away. Maybe the water would wash Hans's kisses off Sarah's lips.

Elder Caldwell started the service with a prayer. Pa looked solemn as Elder Long led him down into the pond. He stood straight up as the elder said a prayer, then bent his knees and went right under as Elder Long laid him in the water. He came up the bank without a shake or a shiver, although the water must have been cold. The joy on his face told me all I had to know about his state of mind.

Ma handed him a quilt and then took her turn next, and came up smiling and praising God. Then Sarah, looking like a wooden soldier, marched into the water. She seemed to have a bad moment when, after his prayer, Elder Long put his hand behind her shoulders to lower her into the water. She pulled away a bit, like a turtle shrinking from the world, struggled a little as she was submerged, and then popped out of the water, shivering. I hoped her sins wouldn't stay on the surface and cling to me. I sure didn't hanker to have Hans

Stiles' kisses stuck anywhere on my hide.

The minute I entered the water, I knew something special was happening to me. Elder Long held his arm up and called me by name, and a sort of glow went through my insides. I wasn't worried anymore about Sarah's sins, and could hardly wait to shed my own.

Then I was under, and up, and felt like a weight was off me, even though the water was cold and I shivered quite a bit.

I climbed out onto the bank and took the blanket Ma gave me. It was John's turn, and I figured he didn't have as many sins to get rid of as I had. Soon the baptism service would be over, but I hoped the wonder of being cleansed would stay with me forever.

Sarah faded into the willows alongside the bank, and I thought I heard muffled sobbing. *Hans sure does have a hold on that girl*, I thought. *Sounds like her heart is broke.*

Mom noticed the sounds Sarah made and went to hunt for her in the trees. I guess she spoke a few words to her, for Sarah quieted down, but I don't think my sister said anything to Ma about the fear and trembling Hans Stiles laid on her about Mormons. Sarah hadn't made much of a fuss about becoming a Mormon herself. To my way of thinking, it was too late now for her to carry on.

I didn't believe what Hans had said, about Mormons having horns and tails. That was ridiculous. I was fast getting to be a real Mormon, and I didn't feel any stubs poking through my skull bones. There surely was no tail in *my* trousers.

As soon as John came out of the water and raised a whoop of joy, he waded out of the pond and Pa put a blanket around him. Elder Long—mostly frozen I expect—also worked his way up the bank and joined Elder Caldwell to receive a blanket of his own.

We all dried ourselves as best we could without a fire. Pa

proposed building one, but Elder Long said a fire would draw attention. Pa nodded.

"Gather round and we'll have the laying on of hands," Elder Caldwell directed.

We all stood around a stump. Pa sat, then the elders put their hands on his head and confirmed him a member of the Church of Jesus Christ of Latter-day Saints. They gave him the Holy Ghost to be with him, and then it was Ma's turn.

Sarah said she wanted to be last, so I went next. I felt a sensation like heat come into my head from the elders' hands, and it joined with the glow that was still in my insides. I felt warm inside, even after my turn in the water, and I knew I was doing the right thing, though I didn't know all about the church. In the days ahead, I figured Pa would teach us what he had learned. That was good enough for me.

After John's confirming, Sarah was persuaded to seat herself on the stump. Her eyes looked kind of wild, but she shivered and shook in silence as Elder Caldwell voiced the prayer of confirmation.

Now we were Mormons. Elder Caldwell asked Pa to close the service with prayer, which he did in a brief word of thanksgiving. As soon as he said "Amen," I was eager to get home and in front of the fire. I think the elders wanted to leave the place, too. They had mentioned the possibility of opposition. I figured nobody knew about our plans, unless Sarah had somehow told Hans, but none of us wanted any problems with the neighbors.

August was far gone. The night air had been nippy enough to chill us as we walked home wearing damp clothing, so the fire at home felt just right. We all gathered around it, even the elders. After a while, I got warm enough on the outside to match the glow inside.

Once we all warmed up sufficiently, we knelt in front of the hearth and had our nightly prayers. Instead of lighting the lamps afterward to read from the Bible or the Book of

Mormon, Pa bid us all go to bed.

I got out of my clothes, laying them on the bedroom furniture with the hope that they would dry before morning. Then I climbed in beside John and whispered my good nights.

"Lije?"

"What?"

"Do you feel good?"

"Sure do."

"Sarah doesn't. What ails her?"

I thought about it a moment. "I suppose she didn't listen too well to the elders' preaching. I don't think she believes."

"Pa and Ma believe."

"I feel so good I'm sure I believe, too."

"I feel good, inside here." He tapped his chest. "'Night, Lije."

"Goodnight, John." I knew what he meant.

Chapter 3

The next morning, I was late to breakfast due to a recalcitrant cow that kicked over the milk pail and soaked my trouser legs. Forced to clean up and change into my next-best work trousers, I came down the ladder from the loft to find the elders still with us, although I thought they had intended to leave early. Evidently Pa had prevailed upon them to stay for breakfast before they undertook their journey.

I figured Pa hesitated to part company with the men who had taught him new doctrines and brought enlightenment to his seeker's mind and heart from new scripture. I didn't know if he felt worried about his capacity to lead his family down new paths or not. My pa was a strong, confident man, and I had no doubt that he could do the job, even though the elders could not remain with us. After all, he had sat for many hours, asking questions and learning everything they could teach him.

Everyone was just sitting down to the table when I came into the room. Although I had missed the blessing on the food, that omission did not keep me from tucking into Ma's golden-brown griddle cakes slathered with fresh butter and dusted with brown sugar, or my ham slice topped with eggs.

Elder Caldwell paused from eating his own meal long enough to tell Pa about a few other families in a wide area of Pennsylvania who had joined themselves to the Church. He mentioned a religious service was held regularly in a town two days travel away. Pa had the elder write down the particulars.

Elder Long glanced at each of us over a forkful of eggs. He took the bite and chewed, still looking around the table. Once he'd cleared his mouth, he said that we were now "Saints of God." We should take every opportunity to gather ourselves together with other church members to strengthen our faith and knowledge until we were ready to journey to Zion—to Nauvoo, the beautiful place—to join the rest of the Saints.

Sarah looked up, concern sharp on her features. From the way she hunched her shoulders, I figured she had in mind Hans's vile words about the evil ways of the Mormon leaders. No doubt she'd believed him when he told her that they sought young wives even after they had a harem of twenty-five or so. Stark fear flickered across her face. I wanted to tell her Hans had fed her a load of hogwash. I did not, because I remembered I'd be in trouble for eavesdropping on her.

I could scarcely put credence in such bald lies about the leaders of our new religion. Who would need more than one wife? Even at my tender years of budding manhood, knowing a time would come when I would want a wife, I had no thought of taking more than the customary allotment. My father's example of kindly, solicitous treatment of my mother made it unthinkable that a man would have such unseemly appetites. I forgot about Hans Stiles' rumors of too many wives and hunkered down to eat the rest of my breakfast.

Then an errant thought struck me. *Journey to Zion?* I raised my head and stared at Elder Long. Somehow, during the past two days, I had missed the expectation of the elders that sooner or later we would leave our home and move ourselves to Illinois. They meant for us to go to that heaven on earth beside the Mississippi River.

Perhaps I was mistaken. I searched my memory. Elder

Long had spoken aloud. I was sure of that. Then Sarah had reacted to his words. Yes, he had mentioned gathering ourselves to Zion. Throughout the visit, he'd spoken of the beautiful city the Saints called Nauvoo.

I looked at Pa, but his air of calm told me nothing. Ma had a secret smile playing about her mouth. What was I to make of that?

The elders had continued giving us counsel, but I had lost the thread of their advice. I fell back to the wild notion of leaving the farm.

It was unthinkable. This was the only home I'd ever had, the only heaven on earth I knew. Pa had given me a field, a beginning for my future. How could I leave that behind and take a step into the unknown?

My stomach roiled at the thought, even as my mind tumbled in disarray.

When I stopped swimming in mental confusion long enough to pay attention again, Elder Caldwell was saying to Pa, "Take the lead in guiding your family. Go to the church services as often as you can." He paused to eat the last bite of ham remaining on his plate, and then continued. "You and Elijah can trade off staying behind to care for the farm."

"We've given you the holy priesthood," Elder Long said to Pa in his turn. "You have the authority to administer the Sacrament of the Lord's Supper to your family when you cannot attend, but you must learn how to do that, so go to the meeting as often as you can manage."

This "holy priesthood" given to my father, and his right thereby to give us a "sacrament," was news to me. I must have missed learning about such rights during the hours I had spent in the fields.

The minister of the church in town had not offered us more than preaching in the services to which I was accustomed. He'd never mentioned a sacrament. His services only included preaching and hymns. "Rock of Ages." "When I

Survey the Wondrous Cross." "A Mighty Fortress is Our God." Hymns and preaching. Heaven and Hell. Fire and brimstone. The fear of God. I'd learned those subjects well. I knew nothing of the Lord's Supper.

When had the elders handed Pa the priesthood? Had Elder Caldwell made some kind of certificate out of the note he scribbled about the location of the church service?

I realized that the coming of the elders had changed more of our lives than I had imagined possible. Now they were leaving us alone. My increasing feeling of panic boiled toward overcoming my usual sense of well-being. What was to become of my family in this strange, new world of Mormondom?

I took a deep breath, followed by a second, and looked up in time to catch my father's smile, which radiated peace. As soon as I saw it, I experienced a wave of calm assurance entering my body at the crown of my head. It continued through to the soles of my feet. My mind ceased its turmoil. My tensed muscles relaxed. All would be well, as my father often told us.

I still didn't know much about my new religion, but I had regained the feeling I'd had last night after my baptism. For now, it was enough.

~ ~ ~ ~ ~

After breakfast, the elders took their leave. Although the day was advancing, minute by minute, we all stood outside the front door and waved to them as they departed. All except Sarah.

She'd headed for the kitchen with a stack of plates after we'd finished the meal, but she hadn't come out with us to bid the elders farewell. I wondered if she'd been as frightened as I'd been by what Elder Long said about going to Zion, or if she had something else on her mind. I couldn't spend much time worrying myself about my sister. I had chores to do, and the sun hadn't stopped its progress across the sky to wait for good-byes.

I'd finished cultivating the field corn in my own plot, but there were other fields that needed my attention. I grabbed the lunch pail Ma had prepared for me, hauled a bucket of water from the well, and took my favorite farm horse, Old Tom, out of his stall, leaving Bess for my father. I rode the horse down the lane to the back forty acres of our land and hitched him to the plow I'd left there yesterday.

The day was hot, and in my haste to get to the field, I'd forgotten my hat. I wasn't in any particular hurry to raise dust from the plowshare into my eyes and nose, so I took my time, lazily following Tom down the rows. Even so, the handles of the plow sent enough shock into the muscles of my arms that I had no fear of falling asleep at my task.

Halting Tom at the end of a row, I wiped the sweat from my eyes with my sleeve, then squinted upward at the sun heading toward the top of the sky. Almost time to eat. Today Ma had packed me a lunch, since I would be out here on the back forty. I wondered if she'd made ham sandwiches. Perhaps my meal was cold chicken, instead. Whatever it was, I knew I'd savor the food, for my mother's cooking never failed to please.

I thought of her dill pickles, and hoped she'd included one. My mouth watered. I could almost taste the sharp flavor and succulent meat of one of my favorite treats. Only a few more rows to till, then I'd investigate the contents of my pail, which I had tucked with the water bucket under a tree at the margin of the field.

When I clucked old Tom into motion again and made the turn into the next row, I noticed clouds gathering atop the low hills on the horizon. The prospect of rain on the dry fields was surely welcome, but if Tom and I hadn't finished with the field before a storm swept over the land, we'd be plowing mud.

As a consequence, I pushed the horse faster than before. The clouds climbed rapidly into the brilliant blue of the sky, and I had six more rows to finish.

We almost beat the weather, but the patter of drops on the stiff leaves of the corn stalks came as a prelude to the rush of warm rain that hit Tom and me with two rows lacking completion.

I drove Tom hard to finish the field, although his coat cascaded with water and my hair did, as well. He didn't seem to mind the downpour when I wrestled the plow out of the mud and unhitched him to find shelter or graze, as he would.

My clothes clung to my skin, weighing far more than they did when dry. I ran in water-filled shoes toward the tree where I had deposited my meal. As I approached, I scanned the sky for lightning. Seeing none, I found a place under the tree and took a seat on the grass and leaves.

After I dumped the water out of my shoes, I peeled off my shirt to wring it out and hung it on a limb under the tree's canopy. I slicked my hands down my trousers to remove as much moisture as possible. Then I opened my lunch pail.

The item on top was a large square of buttered cornbread. I didn't take the time to remove the food and spread it out on the wet grass for inspection, but ate my way to the bottom of the pail, through the cornbread, the eagerly anticipated pickle, three slabs of naked ham, and a slightly warm potato. By the time I felt my hunger abate, the rainfall had begun to slacken. Even so, I couldn't do any more work in this muddy field, so I decided to take the horse back to the barn.

I put on my shirt and shoes, capped up my lunch pail, and made a coil of the sodden leather lines hanging from the harness. I took a long drink of water from the bucket, then I tugged Tom away from his grassy feast and headed home.

When I passed the field where my father had designed to spend his time, I didn't see him. Old Bess was also not in sight. Perhaps Pa had abandoned work earlier than I had. But then I noticed Pa's plow overturned between the furrows, and several of the corn stalks scattered about as though ripped from the ground by an angry hand. The sight puzzled me. My good-tempered parent would not do this to his crop.

I dropped my hold on Tom and ventured as far into the field as the disturbed place. What I hadn't been able to see before gave me pause. The corn stalks had been snapped. There was no way to save those plants. Anger bloomed and heated blood started a headlong rush to my head as I clenched my fists.

"What's going on?" I muttered, and continued to look around. Now I saw that more than one pair of shoes had made the prints in the mud here. Signs of a scuffle all around me, my anger turned to concern for my father's welfare as I decided he had been attacked.

Who had a grudge against Pa? I had no notion. He had always tried to get along with our neighbors, and this vicinity was mostly inhabited by peaceable folk. What could have changed that?

A cold chill flashed down my spine as I grasped hold of the thought that this might be the work of Hans Stiles. Hans and his lay-about companions.

~ ~ ~ ~ ~

I followed a great many footprints in the mud that led through the cornfield. When the trail began to include parallel drag marks, my heart froze. Someone held my father captive. I had no idea of his condition. Was he injured? I halted as a terrible notion struck my mind. Was he dead?

I began to run, heedless of the corn stalks my flailing arms might knock about. The path of prints drew me onward. I followed it to the edge of the field, and then saw that it turned down the line of the fence toward the house. I stared in horror, my chest heaving, to see a crumpled heap of clothing in the corner of the field, a crumpled heap that had no business being there. Stunned, nauseated, I nevertheless made my feet carry me toward the object that lay so still.

As I drew near, it became clear that the bundle of clothing near the fence was indeed my father. "Pa!" I cried out, and continued toward him. My heart caught as he stirred, weakly moving an arm.

I knelt at his side and bent over his form. One cheek bore a swelling purple bruise. The opposite eye wouldn't open again today, I figured. His lip was split, and blood trickled through his hair above one ear. His limbs seemed unbroken, but I wouldn't know that for sure until I investigated further. Even in view of his obvious need for a thorough examination, I was reticent to lay hands upon my father's body.

He caught me about the wrist with one hand, whispering, "Lije. Help me up."

That, I could do. "Pa, what happened?" I asked first, trying to discover how I might manage to raise him without giving him further injury.

"Two," he managed to get out. "Masked."

"Did you know their voices?" I wondered if I could lift and carry him all the way to the house. I didn't want to risk pushing a broken rib into a lung.

"Young men," he said. "Didn't know the sound of them."

That was no wonder, from the blow he'd taken to his ear. From the way he mumbled, I wondered if his jaw was whole. "Where are you hurt the worst?" I asked, pretty sure I knew who at least one of the attackers could be.

"Head. Hit me. With a club. From behind." He paused to get his breath. "Punched my face. My ears."

I saw bruises on his forearms where his shirt sleeves were folded up. He'd probably tried to cover his head with them, and taken cracks from weapons wielded by Hans and his follower.

"Didn't break. My ribs."

Still, he wheezed. He'd taken plenty of punishment, but if he said his ribs were whole, I could lift him.

I set about gathering him into my arms, striving to be

gentle, although my blood boiled to see how my father had been beaten. I staggered under his weight as I got one foot under me and pushed up until I had the second unbent as well and could stand. Pa was not a frail-built man, but I was young, and my anger gave me sufficient strength to carry him in my arms back to the house.

Ma gave a cry as I stumbled through the kitchen door with my burden. She swept the top of the work table free with one arm. As a wooden bowl of rising bread and various tools clattered onto the floor, she demanded that I lay Pa down.

I put him atop the flour-dusted surface and stepped back to let my mother move to his side. Mud from the field flaked off his clothing. Dried blood thickened his hair.

"Sarah!" she screamed for my sister, but I moved to block the door when my sister rushed from the parlor in answer to our mother's call. I didn't want her anywhere near Pa before I could determine if she was complicit in the attack.

"I'll do this," I said to Sarah, and loudly enough for Ma's benefit, too.

Sarah frowned and tried to peer around me, but I put a hand on her shoulder and she looked up at me. Upon seeing the fierce scowl I bent her way, she shrank back, taking in a quick breath.

"You stay away," I muttered at her. She backed up, looked at me again, and turned away into the other room, huddling into herself.

I closed the door, leaned against it for an instant, then pushed myself toward the table upon which lay my father. "What do you need, Ma?"

Chapter 4

By the time the household awoke the next day, I hadn't yet cornered Sarah, so I made it my business to do so before breakfast. Milking the cow could wait half an hour. Finding out if my sister had conspired to injure or kill our father could not.

I came down the ladder from the dim loft room I shared with John and peered into the kitchen. The edge of a brown skirt slid through the closing outside door. My sister must be going to gather eggs.

I caught up in the muddy dooryard and stopped her with a hand on her elbow. She made a little squeaking sound, as though I had startled her, and whirled around, dropping her egg basket.

"Lije—" she started to say, her face white as paste.

"Look here," I cut her off, feeling my anger rise. "Pa's hurt bad enough to be laid up for a couple of weeks or more. What part did you play?"

She shook her head. "None."

"But you know who did it. I can see you do."

She kept shaking her head, her eyebrows drawn together so tightly that her normally smooth forehead looked like a freshly cultivated garden patch. "No," she moaned. "I didn't know—"

"Didn't know what?" I was so angry at having to drag the story out of her that I wanted to strike her. She must have seen my gathering storm, for she shrank away from me, making herself as small as possible.

"Please, Lije. I didn't think he would do anything. He only wanted to know about the baptism."

"Stiles?"

She nodded.

"Pa mentioned two men. Who helped him?"

"I don't know. We were alone when we talked."

"Were you kissing him?"

I don't know where the question came from. That was none of my business. Only the attack on Pa mattered now.

Her face turned from white to red, and I knew I had crossed the line of propriety. I put up my hands in a gesture of surrender. "Was he angry as you spoke?" I asked, trying to turn away her wrath.

Sarah took a long breath and let it out slowly. "He was not," she answered. "He was . . . courtly."

So she probably *was* kissing Stiles, judging from the encounter I had spied upon recently. I restrained my impulse to make a fitting retort and wondered how I was to proceed. She had denied any plotting on her part.

"Has he threatened anyone? You? Pa?"

"He doesn't like the Mormon men who visited us." Her voice barely rose above a whisper. "He didn't want me to join with them."

I already knew that from the conversation I'd overheard. "Did Stiles speak ill of Pa for deciding we would take the baptism?"

"No."

She wouldn't meet my gaze. She was lying. "Sarah? Tell me the truth."

She sniffed, turning her face away.

"Sister."

"He said Pa was making a sore mistake, that he was leading us astray, out of the fold of God."

I made a rude noise and half turned to spit my derision. Since when did Hans Stiles concern himself with God? He had no part of His fold. Instead, he acted the part of a rough character every day, notwithstanding his careful seduction of my sister.

"I think he's right, Lije."

I turned back to stare at Sarah. I knew she had reservations, but she had not refused the baptism, nor the laying on of hands.

She broke contact with my eyes by bending to retrieve her basket from the muddy ground.

I cleared my throat. "I believe what the elders told us. What I heard of it."

"Hans told me of the visitors' evil schemes." Her eyes widened.

I imagined she was recalling his tales. "He told you made-up stories, Sarah. I didn't sense evil in the elders."

She held her peace, but I could tell she didn't agree with my opinion.

"Pa is a good man," I added. "He puts his trust in the Lord. He wouldn't fall for such as Stiles told you." I stopped short as she narrowed her eyes. I'd best quit before she discovered my spying ways.

I waved a hand. "Pa didn't deserve a beating," I said.

"I'm sorry. I didn't know he'd be hurt."

"I'm sorry, too. Hans Stiles isn't the man for you, Sarah. He loves violence too much."

I could tell from her face that she didn't believe me, but I knew my supposition of the man's guilt was correct. For now, I would not question her further. The day was getting on, and I had chores to do.

~ ~ ~ ~ ~

When I went in to lunch, I paused in the doorway to inhale the pleasant odors of the soup simmering in a kettle. Sarah was the only person in the kitchen, so I said to her, "Smells good."

She glared at me as though I'd insulted her cooking.

I wondered if it was the right time to try and make amends for questioning her so sharply this morning, but her scowl was fierce enough that I doubted my ability to get through her anger just now. I shrugged and went through the kitchen to check on my father's state of health.

As I suspected, I found Ma in the bedroom, seated beside the bed, holding Pa's hand. The door was open, but I tapped my knuckles against the door jamb just the same.

"Lije," my mother acknowledged me, beckoning me to enter.

"How is he?" I asked, my voice hushed. A fresh bandage encircled his head. It wasn't the same untidy wrapping I had applied yesterday before I went back outside to bring in the horses.

"In some amount of pain from his ribs," she answered. "He won't be working today."

"Now, Emily," Pa protested from the pillow. "You're coddling me overmuch."

"As if you didn't need a fair bit of coddling," she replied. "Those ruffians did you damage. Who were they?"

Pa gave a minute shake of the head. "I can't name them." He paused to draw a shaky breath. "They wore masks and came upon me from behind." This time he paused for two careful breaths. "I told you that, wife."

From his halting manner of speech, Pa's ribs indeed gave him trouble. I wished I could take away his pain and bear it myself, but even as pangs of sympathy flowed through my body, I could not relieve his suffering one smidgen. At least I could make my suspicions known to my mother.

"I believe Hans Stiles and his bunch are involved," I said. "He's taken an interest in Sarah." I stopped myself from saying anything about the lying tales he had spun for her, knowing I'd be in trouble for spying on my sister, no matter that it had been inadvertent. After all, I *had* continued to listen to their conversation in the henhouse after I knew who was with Sarah. And I'd watched their amorous embraces.

A sort of energy pulsed in my body, a feeling new to me that caught me unaware. Under its unfamiliar influence, I cast my thoughts over the girls my age in the vicinity.

Samantha Calhoun. She had a wall-eye. I'd spent a fair amount of time watching it wander about as she sang in the choir at church, but could I live all my life looking at the spectacle? No. Cordelia Brock. Fair-haired and growing into womanhood well. I could take notice of her. Tilly Kressler. We boys called her Silly Tilly for good reason. Her giggle was overdone. Henrietta Lea—

Ma brought me back to the situation at hand with a quiet, "I knew she was daydreaming far too much these last weeks." She rose, patting Pa's hand before she laid it gently on the quilt. "Let's see if her mind has wandered off her cooking."

"She has a pot of soup going," I said, backing out of Ma's way as she advanced upon the doorway. "It smells nearly edible."

Ma raised an eyebrow. "You must stop teasing your sister."

"I wasn—"

"You do it often, Lije. The day will come when you will regret treating her lightly."

I doubted it, but, with a half-hearted grin and a nod, gave my mother the benefit of her experience, and then followed her into the kitchen.

~ ~ ~ ~ ~

Lunch was a strange affair, with Pa and Ma absent from the table. We had taken our seats without the benefit of our parents' presence. I looked at Sarah, sitting at the head of the table, and waited for her to say grace.

She sat with her eyes downcast. After a long interval in which she made no indication that she would speak a prayer, I glanced around at John and Mary Eliza, cleared my throat, then bowed my head and gave my best imitation of Pa's blessing over the meal.

We ate in silence, for the most part. Even my little sister seemed disheartened by our father's injuries. When had he ever failed to be up and working throughout the day? I sensed that we all felt aimless, lacking the guidance of our good father in our daily activities. Yes, we knew our chores, but the absence of he who cared how well we did them left us with a feeling akin to doom.

At least, that was how I felt.

Mary Eliza began to whimper, wiping her tear-filled eyes with the back of her hand.

"What's the matter, Pumpkin?" I asked.

"Is Papa?" She paused to sniff. "Is Papa going to die?"

"Of course not," I replied, trying to muster an enthusiasm I didn't have. "Ma is the best nurse there is. She'll help him to get well."

My dubious little sister stuck out her bottom lip. "Is you sure?"

"Cross my heart," I said to the accompanying action. I didn't add the rest. I *didn't* hope to die, and I didn't want Mary Eliza thinking any longer of death.

Sarah stirred in her chair. I barely heard her whisper. "It's my fault."

I turned and pegged her to her chair with my frown. "We'll talk later," I muttered. This was neither the time nor the place for an emotional confession. The little one was upset enough.

"You're sure he'll heal up?" asked John from across the table.

I stifled a groan. Was I sure of that myself? "He's down for a couple of days, John, but his life isn't under threat." I hoped my words were true.

I sopped up the remains of the soup with my last morsel of bread, stuffed it into my mouth, and looked at my siblings as I chewed. Sarah stirred her uneaten soup. John tapped his bowl with the edge of his spoon. Mary Eliza pulled on her still-protruding bottom lip. I swallowed and sighed, my mind racing for something to distract them from their unhappy state.

Sarah should take charge, I thought. *She's the eldest.* But I was the eldest son, and the role of leader seemed to be thrust upon my head. The weight seemed heavier than I could bear. I needed help, and I didn't know where to get any. My burdened shoulders slumped as I considered the matter.

Pa always turned to prayer when he had a difficulty. Would that same action assist me? There was no doubt in my mind that I couldn't do anything about relieving the minds of my brother and sisters without some scrap of inspiration from heaven.

I took a moment and looked at my hands clenched in my lap. I folded them together and thought a prayer, a plea for counsel. Gradually my mind cleared of turmoil and the words of a hymn came to me in startling clarity.

Was I supposed to sing?

I hesitated a moment more. My voice had only recently finished changing. At least I hoped it had finished. I didn't want to squawk and frighten Mary Eliza with an un-tempered voice.

The little one stared at me, her face a rain cloud. I had to do something.

I cleared my throat and hummed a pitch, then began to sing "Rock of Ages." By the time I got through the line "from Thy riven side which flowed," I realized Sarah had joined me with her clear soprano voice. A few bars into the second verse, John joined in. As we sang the final phrases of the final verse, Mary Eliza attempted to keep up, and calm had been restored to our hearts by the sweet harmony and comforting words. We'd even got through the part about death without cringing.

While we sat basking in the peace of the quiet moments after the end of our singing, I thought a prayer of gratitude. Surprisingly, the strains of the hymn had thrust aside the ill will in my heart toward Sarah. In that moment, I knew Pa would heal and eventually take leadership of our family off my shoulders. That assurance was a great solace to me. Maybe I didn't have to worry about Hans Stiles and his vicious stupidity in attacking Pa. Maybe I could put the burden on God, and go about the task of farming and learning more about the new religion I had so quickly taken to heart.

Chapter 5

On Thursday morning, Ma asked Sarah, John, and me to come into the downstairs bedroom. Pa wanted to speak to us. I glanced at Ma's face as I passed into the room, noting the tense look she made no effort to hide. I felt the clutch of panic squeezing my gut. Was Pa gathering us to bid his final farewell?

As I neared his bedside, I examined his countenance. There was the look of pain therein, but his color was good. I found none of the gray cast that would indicate approaching death. When he spoke, his voice had strength, and I knew relief. Then I quit dithering and paid attention to his words.

"You'll leave at noon tomorrow. I'll give your mother the address of the worship service that Elder Caldwell wrote out for me. Emily, you and Sarah prepare the food required for the journey. John, help your brother get the wagon ready. Sarah, you will stay to care for my needs."

Despite his sorry state, it appeared that Pa wasn't letting any grass grow under his feet before he heeded the elders' counsel to guide his family in its religious course. He was sending us to meet the other Saints so we could learn from them.

Pa looked at me, straight into my soul. "Take good care of your mother, Elijah. Lend a good ear at the service. You must tell me all you hear."

"I'll do that, Pa," I replied, feeling his confidence in me as keenly as though he'd laid his hand on my shoulder.

By the time Pa dismissed us to go about our assigned tasks, Mary Eliza had awakened and gotten herself to the table. She had a cold bowl of porridge before her, into which she had slopped a healthy portion of milk. Her hair hadn't been combed and hung halfway into her face. I chuckled and patted her on the head as I proceeded on my way outside, and felt her squirm under my hand.

"Lije," she protested. "Don't mess my hair."

I squatted to look into her face. "You look beautiful, Pumpkin," I said. "Eat hearty. We're going on an adventure."

"A 'venture, Lije?"

"You'll see tomorrow," I told her, and left her with those teasing words hanging in the air.

John and I did our usual chores that morning. In addition, we worked on the farm wagon to make it ready to carry us over the hilly roads to our destination, and serve to house us, as well.

John finished pounding a nail into a hoop we were adding to support a canvas top, and looked my way. "Do you think the Mormon preaching service will be different from Reverend Silcoe's?"

I took a moment to think while I drove a nail on my side of the wagon. "That's hard to guess. We'll have to wait until we get there to find out."

"Maybe they won't be partial to singing. I liked it when we sang the other day, Lije. It made my tummy feel better."

I grinned at him, and then wrapped my mind around his suggestion. It sobered me. I hoped the Mormon folk liked to sing. Our hymn had comforted us all. After a while, I arrived at words to answer him. "Think on King David and how many psalms he wrote. I believe the Lord God enjoys singing and holy music. At least, I hope He does."

He was quick to agree. "Me, too!"

Before noon rolled around the next day, John and I had packed up the wagon and put both horses in harness. John led them to the front of the house while I went to the kitchen to tell Ma we were ready.

She looked me over. "The clothes you're wearing will do for travel. Did you pack any for Sunday, for the services?"

I slapped my forehead and climbed the ladder to get my Sunday duds. I wrapped them inside my bedding, then performed the same task for John, tying our bundles closed with bits of string. When I'd brought them down to the ground floor, I went to say my good-byes to Pa.

He sat up in bed, propped against two pillows. I wondered if he should be upright, but perhaps he would get into a more restful position once we had left.

At his invitation, I hugged him with care, then shook his hand. I saw a curious hunger in his eyes.

"I wish I were going with you, son. Pay good heed at the preaching." He gripped my hand firmly, then released it. This was the second time he had mentioned my paying attention to what occurred, and I understood now that his hunger was for spiritual sustenance.

"I will, Pa," I assured him, and took my leave.

~ ~ ~ ~ ~

Our journey was uneventful, if you were to discount my nervous anticipation of meeting other folk who could instruct me concerning the new beliefs I had embraced. Pa's request that I listen well and tell him all I learned sat heavily upon my mind. Would I learn of strange rituals and practices? Encounter guarded people suspicious of my interest? Or would I find regular folk happy to impart of their knowledge?

Late Saturday afternoon, we made our camp on the outskirts of the town. We had not brought any tenting material. The weather was still pleasant enough that John and I would sleep under the wagon as we had on Friday night. Ma had made a comfortable place in the wagon box, so she and Mary Eliza would again sleep under the canvas top.

Ma asked me to offer our prayer that night, which I did, using as much of Pa's customary language as I could cram into it, including an expression of gratitude that all had gone well during our journey. At the end, I remembered to petition God on behalf of Pa's recovery and his and Sarah's safety in our absence. The addition felt strange in my mouth, an awkward departure from the bounds prescribed by my father's example. I took the stumbling step, however. In light of the attack upon Pa, it seemed the better part of caution that I ask for God's hand of protection for all members of the family.

I spent a nervous night under the wagon, anticipating my meeting with strangers. In truth, my family and I would be the interlopers, but that thought did not calm my anxiety. At last the dawn came, and with it, the Sabbath day. I ate the food Ma gave me, but it sat upon my stomach like a lump of rock: undigested and indigestible.

We left our camp nearly forty-five minutes before the appointed hour for the meeting, in case we should get lost. I had worked myself into quite an unsettled condition by the time I pulled the horses to a halt at the appointed street corner.

We had arrived in the center of the town. The streets were practically deserted, cloaked in an appropriate stillness for the Lord's Day. However, I could see no building resembling a church.

"Are we there, Lije?" Mary Eliza called from the back of the wagon.

I groaned inwardly. She had asked that same question time and time again during our travels. I wondered how Pa stood her infantile questions.

"I'll find out, Pumpkin."

I looked from one building to the next, seeking to verify that we had come to the correct intersection in the city. Ma, who sat beside me on the wagon seat, looked as puzzled as I felt. She glanced at the paper in her hand, furrowed her brows, and nodded to me.

We were at the right location, but the directions we had been given had brought us to a saloon.

I stood and surveyed the four corners of the intersection. I was mistaken. I counted one, two, three, four saloons, each one firmly planted on its own corner.

"This cannot be correct," I muttered, wrapping the lines around the brake handle. "I'll go ask where the Mormon's church house is to be found." I vaulted to the ground and looked around for a friendly face I might approach for guidance.

A sandy-haired man dressed in his Sunday best, accompanied by a woman and four children, came into view from around a corner, walked past us, then stopped before the saloon closest to us. He pulled a ring of keys from his pocket.

Surely he wasn't taking his family into that den of iniquity?

Sure enough, he unlocked the door, opened it, and headed inside.

Perplexed by his actions, I looked for another avenue for enlightenment, but none was at hand. Needing information, I sidled toward the man and his family, who were filing after him through the doorway.

I caught up to him inside the saloon. "I beg your indulgence," I said. "Might you give me directions?"

"Certainly, brother," he replied, which I thought was a strange greeting.

"I'm looking for the Mormon edifice."

"Edifice?"

Perhaps I hadn't imagined a grand enough structure. I tried again. "Cathedral?"

"Oh, you're looking for their meeting place."

"Yes, I—"

"You've found it, lad."

"What? Here?" I looked around the bar room in confusion. A depiction of a wanton woman hanging behind the bar caused me to blush.

The man chuckled as the woman I presumed to be his wife handed him a covered basket. "Yes. We have no building of our own, so we rent the saloon. It's closed on Sundays, you know."

"You're a Mormon?"

"Indeed, I am." He stuck out his hand and grasped mine. "Ralph Peters, at your service. I'm the branch president here."

"Branch president?" I shook his hand, wondering what the words signified.

He must have guessed at my confusion. "I'm the local leader. Are you of our faith?"

"Newly baptized," I told him, and pointed toward the door. "My mother and my brother and sister are outside. The elders said we were to come here to meetings."

He nodded and placed the basket upon the bar. As he took off his hat and coat and began to roll up his shirtsleeves, I shifted my gaze sideways at the bottles lined up behind the bar and noticed that a piece of cloth had been draped over the painting, thankfully covering the nakedness of the soiled woman.

I looked further around the room. A young man of about my age and his younger brother were engaged in stacking the tables in a corner. Bright red hair peeked out from under their caps. A girl nudged a chair into a row. Her braids were not red, but a pleasing yellow color.

Evidently ready to engage in more conversation, Mr. Peters said, "When they last stopped by, Elders Caldwell and Long mentioned they had made converts of several families out in the county. Did your father not come?"

"He's laid up with injury," I said. "My older sister is tending to him. He thought it important that we come."

"And rightly so," Mr. Peters said. "Saints must gather together for strength, particularly hereabouts."

Remembering my manners, I gave my name, and that of my mother and siblings.

"Well now, young Brother Marshall, bring in your family and help us make the place decent. We'll begin on the hour."

I accordingly went to fetch my family members. Ma hesitated to enter a saloon, but I explained that I had met the local leader and there was no Mormon church building, so rented facilities must serve.

She took Mary Eliza by the hand in a firm grasp, inhaled until I thought her lungs must burst, and then marched into the building, trailed by John, who shot me a questioning look.

"I don't think there are very many Mormons in Pennsylvania, even here in town," I whispered, falling into step with him. "I imagine it takes a large congregation to raise enough cash to construct a building."

He made a sound I took as meaning he understood the circumstances, but in truth, I wasn't sure I fully understood everything, myself. My wonderment didn't prevent me noticing his eyes going wide at his first look at a saloon. I figured it would be the topic of our nightly conversations for at least a month to come.

A woman and an older girl came up to Ma and greeted her quite cordially. Seeing that she and Mary Eliza were in good hands, I looked about for a task to accomplish, sent John off to do the same, and joined the older boy in carrying a table to what evidently had been designated as the "front" of the room. I supposed it would act as the pulpit or altar, but the boy, who had introduced himself as Paul Peters, spread a white linen cloth over the surface, then asked, "Have you been ordained?"

I didn't think so, whatever "ordained" meant, and responded in the negative.

"Then let me do this," he said. "You watch and learn. Once you're ordained to the priesthood, you'll have ordinances to perform, too."

Ordained to the priesthood. Ordinances to perform. Right away, I had received enlightenment. The holy priesthood the elders had mentioned they gave Pa had not been imparted by a scrap of paper. They must have ordained Pa before breakfast on the day they'd left, on the day I'd been delayed by an untimely milk bath. I wondered if that unruly cow had prevented me from being ordained, as well.

Paul laid a slice of bread on a plate, poured water into a small glass tumbler, and then covered the bread and water with another cloth. "This is for the Sacrament of the Lord's Supper, which we will observe during the meeting," he explained. "Listen close to the prayers said over the emblems. They will help you remember the time of your baptism. Mine was over a year ago."

I made a mental note of Paul's actions in preparing for the rite—and his unfamiliar words—before I recounted to him my baptismal experience. We settled into an easy conversation. Paul was congenial, and I liked having a friend. What a contrast he was to Hans Stiles and his cronies.

~ ~ ~ ~ ~

By and by, the Peters family and mine, accompanied by several more Saints who had arrived, turned the bar room into the semblance of a place fit for the Lord to enter. More Mormon Saints entered the room, and true to Mr. Peters' word, the meeting commenced on the hour.

Paul had instructed me in the proper form of address amongst the Saints, so I now understood that his father was to be called "President" Peters. The church members were properly called "Saints," not "Mormons," and I was to address them as "Brother" this or "Sister" that. "But I'll answer to plain 'Paul'," he'd said, chuckling.

President Peters—by now restored to proper dignity by donning his coat and hat—called for our attention by rising from where he had been sitting at the front with two other men, on chairs facing those of the other Saints. He announced that we would sing a hymn called "The Morning Breaks, The Shadows Flee," and commenced to lead the group with a hand motion and his strong voice. Although a piano sat shoved into a corner, no one ventured to accompany the hymn.

I was glad to learn that the Saints did sing hymns, even though I didn't know the words or the tune to this particular one. By the time the members had sung five verses, though, I was getting the hang of it.

Next, President Peters called upon one of the gentlemen in the congregation to pray, and pray he did, for some length of time. I opened one eye to a slit, hoping for some sign that the man was winding up what, by this time, had almost amounted to an entire sermon. Just then, the man paused, and I caught sight of President Peters tugging on his coat tail. He whispered, "Enough, Brother Barnes," after which our Brother Barnes made quick work of wrapping it up. It seemed to me that the "Amens" afterward had several tangible sighs of relief affixed.

Next, President Peters gave a list of announcements, including the birth of a bouncing baby boy to the Pospisil family, and the poor condition of the health of Sister Friedrich, asking for private prayers to be offered in her behalf. My head was swimming—trying to remember it all to recount to my father—by the time President Peters had finished his announcements and called for my mother to stand up.

She looked at me, fright in her eyes, but she stood, and then, my name and that of John were also called out, and we had to stand inspection, as well.

It turned out not to be an inspection. We were instead received into the body of the Saints, with the members raising their hands to vote that into effect. It felt right to be members of Christ's true fold.

I wondered why Mary Eliza's name hadn't been called, but was somewhat relieved that such was not the case. My little sister might have caused a scene due to fright. I was thankful that she had not had the occasion presented to her to become spooked.

Paul's younger brother, Timothy, was motioned forward. It happened that he had only just had his twelfth birthday, and he was due to have conferred upon him the "Aaronic Priesthood," and the office of "deacon." I observed and listened carefully to all that occurred, as I might someday hear my name called for the same sort of process. I didn't want to make a fool of myself when the time came.

Then we sang another hymn. One of the men sitting beside President Peters took his place behind the table Paul had prepared, lifted the cloth to expose the plate, and tore the bread into pieces. When the hymn-singing had finished, he knelt and offered a prayer that, as Paul had mentioned beforehand, reminded me of the things said at the time of my baptism.

Paul took the plate containing the pieces of bread from the man and offered it to the other men seated at the front, then to each of us, in turn. I took a piece of bread, now designated as the body of Christ, and placed it in my mouth. Although it had been blessed, it tasted the same as my mother's home-baked loaves. I wasn't sure if I was disappointed or relieved. I'd never been offered a representation of the flesh of Christ before, but if eating it helped me remember His goodness and grace toward me, all was well.

Then Paul returned to face the man standing at the table, and offered the almost empty plate to him. The man took a piece of the bread and put it in his mouth, then he took the plate and offered it to Paul. In this manner, all present had received and eaten a piece of bread representative of the body of Christ by which to recall their baptism vows.

After the man laid the plate back in its place, he uncovered the tumbler, knelt again, and gave a prayer over the water. He handed the cup to Paul, who passed it all around the room as he had done with the plate of bread. I noticed that most people turned the glass to a new portion of the rim before they took a sip of the blessed water. Not knowing if this action was part of the ritual or done out of personal preference, I did likewise.

When all had received water signifying the blood of Christ from the tumbler, Paul returned it to the man at the table, and they both sipped from the cup. The brother then put it beside the plate, covered it with the cloth, returned to sit beside President Peters, and that was that.

The next thing I knew, the other man beside the President was asked to preach a sermon. This was new to me. Reverend Silcoe always reserved that right for himself, except for the rare occasion when he was absent for one reason or another, and a visiting preacher had given the sermon.

Brother Halverson, for that was the man's name, preached on the significance of the Sacrament of the Lord's Supper, for which I was glad, as I learned much that had been lacking in my spiritual education.

It seemed he didn't hold forth nearly as long as Brother Barnes had for his prayer. This pleased me, as my nether regions were becoming slightly numb as the meeting continued. I was not a fellow naturally inclined to sit still for extended lengths of time, and I knew John to be of the same stripe.

Just as I was sure the meeting would end, the man who had presided over the Sacrament arose in response to President Peters' call, and launched into a sermon of his own.

By this time, the cells of my brain had started a similar journey toward numbness, and I feared that I would find myself remiss in my mission to report to my father all that had occurred this day.

Fortunately for both my top and my bottom regions, the topic of this man's sermon was the Priesthood, a subject that held my interest. My brain cells enlivened, and I drank in all that he said.

Then we sang another hymn, "Rock of Ages," which I knew well, and I joined in with enthusiasm.

A prayer, mercifully short, ended the service, and I looked forward to our journey home so that I could report. But before I could gather the family and head for the door, President Peters called my name, and beckoned to me. He wished to speak with me, and so we went into a musty back room, where he undertook an interview that seemed to plumb the depths of my soul.

He learned that I was coasting along on the back of my father's beliefs and faith, so he enjoined me to read the Book that the elders had left at our home. I promised to do so, and he said he would talk to me again the next time we came for church services. I know he hoped we would be able to return each Sunday, but I wasn't sure that was possible, with the harvest approaching and Pa needing to heal from his wounds before he could take the lead of our family once more.

With that, President Peters dismissed me, and our weekend's journey of spiritual discovery came to an end. We still had to travel home, but that was a bit of an anticlimax. The meat of the event had been eaten, digested, and remembered. Now we were obliged to return to our work-a-day world.

~ ~ ~ ~ ~

Nearly the first thing I did once we had arrived home was report all the events of the Sabbath services to my father. As I spoke, he sat upright in his bed, transfixed by my words.

It was as though he were truly starving and I had in my mouth the means to cure his hunger. This thrilled me, for some reason, this chance to school my father on a subject previously unknown to him. I had not supposed my report would have this effect on him or on me. On all other reportorial occasions, he had been the father, and I, the son, recounting the results of my task. Now I sensed a shift in our relationship, as though he acknowledged a growth in me, a maturity that I still did not feel I had achieved.

He waited until I had spoken my piece, then he asked me questions, dozens of them.

I answered as best I could, and when I began to fear that he had exhausted himself, he relaxed against his pillows with an immense smile on his lips and gave a gusty sigh. I slumped a bit, but felt a curious elation at having sated his desire for knowledge so satisfactorily.

Pa reached out and gripped my hand. "Thank you, Elijah," he said. "Well done."

The glow that settled over my heart lasted far into the night, and carried me through the next day.

Chapter 6

One day while my father still lay abed, Reverend Silcoe approached me in the field. When he had drawn near, a look of confusion spread across his face, followed by one of resignation.

"It's you," he said, and took a handkerchief from his pocket.

I waited as he wiped the drops of sweat from his brow. When he seemed disposed to speak to me again, I perversely forestalled him by saying, "Pa is up at the house, sir. I'm sure he'll delight in seeing you."

He shook his head at my impertinence and took himself away toward the house.

It being nearly noon, Bess and I followed after him on our way to the barn. After I had put away the horse, I washed up and entered the kitchen.

The sound of a furious voice greeted me, calling upon Heaven to rain damnation upon my father and mother. I assumed the curse was intended to extend to myself and my siblings, which rankled my feelings a good bit. But when I looked over at Sarah, who was staring white-faced toward the sound of the hubbub, I went to her, feeling that I should refute the ugly words in order to bring her comfort.

"He hasn't the right, sister," I said, "nor the power of God to curse us."

"He's a minister," she whispered, her eyes wide and wild.

"But his authority is that of a man," I countered. "Elder Caldwell and Elder Long gave Pa the power of God." I put my arm around her shoulder. "I learned more about that priesthood when we went to the service."

Since our family had not attended the church represented by the incensed man in the other room since our baptisms, I'm sure she knew which service I meant. "I wish you could have attended. Several young ladies came. You would have liked them."

In truth, I had no idea if the young ladies in attendance would have been compatible with my sister, but from the welcome all the members had showered upon my family, I surmised that she would have been included in the warmth of godly love I'd felt.

Sarah shivered within the shelter of my arm. She remained unconvinced.

I squeezed her shoulder. "All will be well," I said, then removed my arm, hoping she believed my words.

I left her in the kitchen, gripping the edge of the work table with white-knuckled hands.

When I got to the hall outside my parents' room, Pa was speaking in a firm, quiet voice.

"You're a good man, Charles, but I've chosen a new path. Your disappointment must not lead you to intemperate words."

He paused, and I expected to hear a protestation from the reverend, but it didn't come. Instead, Pa spoke again.

"My family does not deserve your censure. I reject your call for Heaven's damnation of us. We are walking in a good road, and all will be well."

I realized in that moment that I had copied my assurance to Sarah from my father's consistent words of encouragement.

I heard the scrape of chair legs being pushed across the floor. Glad of the warning, I hastened into the parlor and sat, pulling the Bible onto my lap. I got it open before Reverend Silcoe stormed into the room and out the front door. I let him go without a peep to stop him. If he had such a poor opinion of us, far be it from me to impede his exit from our home. It was going to be hard to forget the anger engraved on his face, though. For a man of God, he surely had a temper.

~ ~ ~ ~ ~

A few days later, Ma sent John to town with a basket of eggs to trade for a few pounds of sugar at the general store. He returned later than he should have, eggs smeared on his clothing and in his hair. One of his eyes sported significant swelling and bruising. I followed him into the kitchen.

Ma cried out and bent down to grasp his chin in her fingers. Turning his face from side to side, she checked him for additional damage. "What happened, son?"

"Mr. Green wouldn't trade with me, Ma. I was on my way to the McFate's when the Green boys . . . stopped me," he said.

"You fought with them?" I asked.

"They started it," he mumbled through the washing cloth with which Ma was cleaning his face.

"I hope you gave as good as you got," I said.

He didn't answer me on that score. Instead, he muttered, "The reverend preached against us, Ma. Sam Green said he was only doing his Christian duty."

"Well, Sam Green's ma is going to get a piece of my mind," Ma said, releasing John's chin.

"It was his Pa's doing," John protested. He rubbed his cheek where the imprint of Ma's fingers remained. "I guess it didn't even start there," he added. "The preacher started the whole thing, speaking out against us."

Ma sighed. "You could say we started it." She straightened up, holding her shoulders high. "We joined God's true church, but that ought not bring such unchristian treatment down upon us."

I agreed with her assessment, but didn't say anything.

"You'll need a good scrubbing to get that egg out of your hair," Ma continued. "Go draw a couple of buckets of water, and I'll heat the boiler." She gestured toward the water reservoir on the stove.

"Oh, Ma. It's not Saturday night."

"No, but you'll thank me come bedtime."

"Can't I just use a bucketful of water and scrub up in the barn?"

Seeing that John had come to no lasting harm, I left him to try his best persuasions with our mother, and went back outside to finish my chores.

~ ~ ~ ~ ~

By suppertime, John looked like a new man—well, boy at least—with his damp hair combed into submission and the egg residue absent from his person.

Ma said she would sit with us at the table that night. She told John he was to take the tray into Pa's room to explain his altercation and help Pa eat, if he needed any assistance.

Before we sat down to supper, I looked in on Pa. He looked better with the color fading from the bruise on his face and both eyes open. I could tell he chafed at Ma's insistence that he stay in bed, for he wasn't a man to be idle.

"Elijah," he greeted me.

I sat beside his bed and gave him a report on the farm work. When I had finished, he stared into my eyes for a long moment, then nodded.

"You are doing well with the farm, son, but what is troubling you?"

I don't know why I was surprised that he had read me so easily. I took a moment to formulate an answer.

"Reverend Silcoe has added to our woes," I said. "He preached against us on Sunday, according to John." I paused. "I should let him tell the tale. He'll be here shortly with your supper."

"All right. I'll hear him out. You are fretting, Lije."

"I didn't expect folks to beat you and pick on John merely because we chose to join a different church. Ma said the same." I looked down. My fists were clenched so tightly that my knuckles appeared as snow-capped mountains. I eased my hands open and gripped my knees instead.

Pa reached out his hand, and I took it gingerly. "That book the elders left. The Book of Mormon. At the beginning, the prophet Lehi was laughed to scorn because of his belief in God's word. His sons were in danger of their lives when they returned to gather records. Can we expect better treatment?"

I shifted in the chair, guiltily remembering my promise to President Peters to read that book. "I guess not."

Pa nodded. "So it was anciently. So it is today. People sometimes fear truth, especially when it calls for change." He squeezed my hand. "Go to supper, Lije, and give no more worry to the matter."

I left him then and went to eat, trying to let his counsel sooth my fears.

~ ~ ~ ~ ~

Although Pa was making progress in healing, I fretted that harvest was nearly upon us. I sorely needed his guidance and help in bringing in the crops.

Word had spread throughout the countryside that Pa had been injured. From time to time a man or a youth would show up to help me with the chores or to assist me in harvesting a field. I should have shown more faith in the human race, but I felt sorely tried when I thought back to the ill treatment we had received at the hands of some of our neighbors.

I knew I should obey Pa's counsel and let the affronts go, but I was caught up in boyish petulance and was not thinking like the man whose role I had been forced into assuming.

Although I received help in the daylight hours, we also had night predators—human marauders who, on one occasion, stripped a field I had not yet touched. I was devastated at the loss of the corn, stalks hacked down, left in the rows, and ridden upon by horses until the ears were embedded in the earth. I salvaged what little I could, but this had been the most promising field, the field Pa had given me, and which I had nurtured as best I knew how.

I didn't want to burden Pa with the horrendous news, but I couldn't avoid our conversation before supper. Even though the field was mine, its yield was meant to feed our animals throughout the coming winter. With a sick heart, I dragged myself into Pa's room.

He sat upon the edge of the bed, and must have heard my gasp of surprise when I entered.

"Yes, I am joining you at supper tonight. I cannot abide lying here any longer."

He had dressed himself, and now sat, husbanding strength to make the trek to the table.

"Give me your arm, Elijah," he said, and I hastened to do his bidding. I forgot all about the wasted field and my grief at the destruction as I helped my father take his rightful place at the head of the table. There was at last joy in the day. Pa was back!

Chapter 7

Once Pa got out of bed, it seemed that he became a new man, strengthened, more lively, and rapidly regaining all his faculties. I rejoiced. Who could not? Ma's face was more often than not wreathed in smiles, as well. Happiness abounded in our home, and if someone treated us badly from time to time, we could forgive. I could forgive. I had new hope, new heart with Pa's recovery.

Now that Pa worked alongside me in the fields again, I also had the strength at night to begin keeping my promise to President Peters. The stories in the *Book of Mormon* fascinated me; tales of trials worse than mine, but also of perseverance in the face of those trials. And the best part? They were true accounts. I knew that from the moment I began with the opening words, "I, Nephi . . ." This Nephi was not much older than I, perhaps even my own age. Every time I read from the Book, a cocoon of warmth comforted me and gave me a surety that I, too, could overcome adversity.

The day finally came when our crops were out of the fields, put up and safely tucked away to nourish the family and our animals during the cold of winter. Ma and Sarah, with a little help from Mary Eliza, had spent the season laboring in the truck garden, then in the kitchen, harvesting, canning and drying the vegetables. The harvest had been bounteous; the cellar was full; the barn was replete with the work of our hands.

"We will attend services this Sunday," Pa announced at supper. "Jeremiah will look after the animals while we are gone."

Jeremiah was Mr. Rommel, our neighbor but one to the south. He and Pa had a firm friendship that had not slipped because we had foregone the pleasures of Mr. Silcoe's sermons.

My heart leaped. I had only a few pages left to read in the Book. Although the factions were embroiled in a tragic war, I could not help reading further. I had gained a tender shoot of a testimony of God's love for me, and hoped I no longer had to shelter under my father's broad-leafed tree.

Pa smiled. Ma smiled. I smiled. John smiled. Mary Eliza smiled.

Sarah did not smile. Sarah frowned. Sarah sighed and cried and carried on as though Pa had demanded she cut off her hand. I could not imagine how she had been meeting Hans Stiles, as busy as Ma had kept her, but I had no doubt she was still in his thrall.

Pa would not relent. The entire family would go to meeting, and that was the end of the argument.

I could not help sympathizing with Sarah, wrong-minded as her feelings were. She looked so forlorn, creeping around the house like a titmouse until the day we left, with Sarah in the wagon, despite her long face.

~ ~ ~ ~ ~

There were several moments after we arrived when I thought Sarah might have been won over by the welcome we found. She met the young ladies, and seemed to get on well with them. I left her in their tender embraces, and went to help change the saloon into a house of God.

President Peters called me aside. We went into the back room as before, although this interview took place before the meeting commenced. He questioned me about my reading progress. I was delighted to report that I had finished the

Book. I believe he was highly amused by my enthusiastic recounting of my favorite parts. Then he got down to cases and proposed that I receive the priesthood that very day.

That sobered me. I wasn't sure I was up to the challenge, but he reminded me that his young son Timothy was doing well in his responsibilities, and I had a few years on the lad. I was given to understand the difference between my father's higher priesthood and the one I would hold, the same that Aaron of Old and his sons possessed. The president had all confidence that I would do my duties faithfully. He explained what those entailed, and although I had mild feelings of trepidation still, I agreed to his proposal.

And so it was that I became the second in our household to be endowed with power from on high.

My feelings on our journey home soared to the heavens. Pa reveled in having attended the meeting to learn more light and truth. Ma glowed. I knew that was partly because of her condition, showing boldly that our family was increasing in size. Part of it was basking in Pa's happiness, too. She held Mary Eliza close and sang hymns with her. John joined in, his voice clear and true.

Sarah appeared to be content until we were within ten miles of home. At that point, her mood changed. Her eyes filled with tears and her head went down. She made sounds indicative of deep distress. I tried to pay her no mind, as her mood would have pulled mine down had I paid more heed.

When we crested the ridge and entered our valley, the air held a smoky bite. It was like stepping into a smokehouse. I wondered what had occurred in our absence, and I knew Pa was on the alert.

Then, as we passed Jeremiah Rommel's farmstead, the man stepped into the road and called to Pa.

"There's trouble, James," he said in his thick German accent.

Pa pulled up the horses, and Mr. Rommel came to Pa's

side of the wagon and motioned him to descend. They walked off a few paces, so I didn't hear what they discussed, but Pa's sudden cry of "What?" rang in my memory for weeks afterward.

~ ~ ~ ~ ~

The previous day, masked raiders appeared as Mr. Rommel slopped our hogs at dusk, hogs we had planned to butcher soon. The villains pushed Mr. Rommel into a ditch, shot the hogs, killed the chickens, and then fired the barn. Fired the barn! I imagined the frantic lowing of the cows as they pushed against the stout, confining partitions of the stalls, slowly choking on the thick smoke of the burning corn and wheat, and finally roasting to death in the conflagration.

How can I tell of the sorrow, of the overwhelming loss? I cannot bear to recount it. The only glimmer of light amid the smoky pall of destruction was the contents of the root cellar. And yet, we could not survive on vegetables alone. Without the hog meat, the chickens and eggs, the milk and occasional beef, we would starve.

That appeared to be the intention of our foes. There was no credit to be had at the mercantile establishments. We had no surplus foodstuffs to trade for implements to replace the plowshares, hoes, harrows, and other equipment lost in the fire. Harnesses, rope, buckets, barrels, feed—all were gone, and we were left no way to get more.

Pa and I tried to hire ourselves out for any work we could feasibly do. No one with jobs available wanted a Mormon or two working on their place.

On one particularly discouraging day, I reminded my father of the story of young Nephi, who, when his bow lost its spring and his family similarly faced starvation, turned to God for enlightenment. Pa went still for several moments, his face taking on a solemn aspect, and then he agreed that we must use all powers at our disposal. His hand on my shoulder was more praise than words could have said.

We fasted—of necessity, but also with faith and prayer—to find answers to our critical lack of food. Pa finally resorted to using kitchen implements to melt down the pewter candlesticks for shot, while I begged the neighbors for chicken dung so we could manufacture gunpowder. When we had gathered a meager store of both, he and I went hunting, stressed almost to the breaking point by the knowledge that every shot must count. In that manner, I learned to be a marksman.

Using our utmost ingenuity, we crafted snares, and trapped foxes and smaller fur-bearing animals. When we could find no buyers for the skins, we used them to make winter clothing for ourselves.

I shot a deer, and Pa brought down a fat bear that had become a neighborhood nuisance from visiting folks' garbage pits. With the meat portioned out on a strict schedule, we hoped to keep our bodies and souls together until spring.

But long ere spring appeared, grief visited us again, and in an embittering way.

~ ~ ~ ~ ~

Pa and I returned one evening from running our trap lines to find Sarah frantic with worry. Ma, worn from the blow dealt by our neighborhood ruffians and the hard work and worry of making meals for her family from practically nothing, had begun to bleed heavily. Her moans—I could not tell whether from pain or sorrow—filled the house. After hours of agony, she lost the beloved child.

If that wasn't enough, she continued to bleed. No one would come to aid Sarah, who knew next to nothing about such female maladies. The doctor declined to come, citing a previous obligation. I found it hard to believe his excuse, knowing that he was a most fervent member of Reverend Silcoe's flock.

Pa directed me to gather moss, hoping a packing of same would stem the bleeding. Whether or not Sarah carried out

Pa's exhortation correctly, I know not, but she reported a lack of success. On the second day of Ma's crisis, a Quaker lady, a Mrs. Alice Manning, heard of the situation and came to assist. I don't know if Mrs. Manning was disgusted by the lack of "Christian charity" in our neighborhood, or if she had such a kind heart that she could not forebear coming from two valleys away, but after many hours of skillful care, she saved my mother's life.

When the crisis had passed and before she took her leave, Mrs. Manning asked for a conversation with my father, which I overheard from the kitchen.

"Thee must guard that thy wife does not ever carry another child," she began.

I heard nothing for a long moment until Pa's voice came again, in almost a hush. "Emily will take that hard."

"Friend Marshall, the restriction will be cumbersome on thee, as well, but her female system is now not strong enough to bear another child. Thee must be circumspect."

Sorrows upon sorrows.

I thought my mother would never laugh again. She did not arise from her bed until February had come and gone. For the first year since I had memory, the family did not celebrate my birthday at the time called St. Valentine's Day. By the end of the month, even though spring was approaching, our food situation was so dire that we boiled all hides and skins we could obtain to make a thin soup containing whatever fat had adhered to the pelts.

Late one night I awoke to use the chamber pot and heard my mother sobbing to my father that she could no longer bear to live here. The next morning, he presented us with a plan: instead of continuing to figure out how to plant crops this season, at the end of March we would gather to Zion, which meant we would begin a journey to Nauvoo, Illinois, on the banks of the Mississippi River.

Oh, the fuss and feathers that flew over that scheme!

Sarah refused to go, crying the night through and arising with swollen, red eyes and a severe attitude not much mended by sleep. I had no patience with her. Taxed by all that had occurred, even the thought of losing my field did not deter my hope that another place—any place—would be better than this one.

Pa and John and I bore the brunt of carrying out the plan in the limited time until March thirty-first. Ma was still too weak to participate in much of the work, Mary Eliza was too young, and Sarah refused to perform any labor having to do with our removal. Accordingly, Pa tasked me with many kitchen chores. I therefore learned to accomplish many housewifely chores, and didn't regret a minute of it.

John found my cheerfulness in the kitchen to be strange, and ragged me about it unmercifully. I didn't care. I was desperate to get to Zion. If cooking and cleaning up and doing whatever I could to make it possible was unmanly, I simply did not care. Who was to notice? We had no visitors, no nearby kin, no one to wonder at my unnatural education in kitchen skills.

Only one thing chafed me: sharing kitchen time with Sarah. Although I wondered where my former compassion for my sister had gone, I had grown impatient with her constant haranguing against my faith, and her adamant refusal to obey our father. In my mind, she lived under her father's roof; therefore, she owed him obedience.

I don't know when I realized that Sarah was slipping off for hours at a time each day. It pleased me that she was absent. At first I thought she was gathering roots down by the river, or robbing birds' nests for eggs, but it finally occurred to me that her hours away did not increase our food supply. She was doing something else during those hours. I had no time to follow her to see if she snuck off to meet Hans Stiles, and John wouldn't do it, so I decided to leave her to her own devices, after which I shared my suspicions with my father.

Pa shook his head when I told him. "Your sister is making her own choices," he said, his face lined with naked grief.

I thought of Laban and Lemuel in the Book of Mormon, and the grief they had inflicted upon their father. "Then throw her out," I said, and immediately regretted my outburst. "I'm sorry, Pa. I shouldn't have said that, let alone thought it."

"Elijah," he said, "when I see how much pain she gives your mother, I think the same thoughts. Then I repent, because she's our daughter, and I must not treat her unkindly, whatever she may do, whatever vitriolic nonsense she may say."

I nodded, wondering how I could ease my parent's troubles. Perhaps I should treat Sarah more kindly myself. Perhaps kindness could cure her bitterness, and what I suspected was wanton behavior.

I decided I must quit judging my sister and endeavor to increase my love toward her. Didn't the Book preach love? I was sure of it.

~ ~ ~ ~ ~

The day of our departure finally arrived, and, as I suspected would happen, Sarah was nowhere to be found. She had slipped away in the night. I had slept so deeply that I did not hear her arise so I could prevent her action.

All the day, as Pa and I searched for her, I felt the heavy weight of guilt upon my shoulders. Every cruel action, every unkind word I had directed toward my sister came back to haunt me.

As I went from farm to farm, no one would admit to knowing where she could be. Finally, reluctantly, I went to the rundown place where Hans Stiles had made his abode, only to find . . . well, he was gone, too. My heart dropped into my toes, and I walked slowly home, dreading the encounter I must have with my remaining family members.

Ma knew the results of my search the minute I walked into the house. She threw her apron over her head and sobbed into it. I felt no better, aching to throw a protective arm around my sister. Pa sighed. I'm sure his eyes misted. When he burst into tears, John failed in his attempt to act the part of a man. Mary Eliza wailed, "Sister, my sister," when she realized Sarah would not return. A sadder family was not to be found in our valley, which soon would become merely "the valley," and ours, no longer.

We could not spare another day searching for Sarah. We supposed she had fled with Hans Stiles, and our only solace could be to wish that the wretch would be a proper man and marry her.

We set off the next day, sobered and disheartened, yearning for that which we could not have: a united family.

Chapter 8

As our horses plodded westward, a pall of sadness accompanied us. Even though we were relieved to be leaving the place of our oppressions, the loss of Sarah, our sister, my parents' daughter, weighed upon us like a heavy hand.

Ma's face mirrored her feelings with deep lines etched into her forehead. Pa's shoulders drooped uncharacteristically for many days. I missed John's whistle as we walked along behind the slow wagon. Mary Eliza alternated between sobbing and sniffling, wiping her nose frequently with the back of her hand until Ma gave her a small bit of linen cloth to use instead.

My chest ached with remorse. Perhaps if I had treated Sarah with more kindness, more compassion, she would have felt more welcome within our family circle, despite her abrasive attitude and cruel words. Perhaps she would not have chosen to run away with Hans Stiles had my actions been more those of a follower of Christ than of a self-righteous, know-it-all younger brother.

I felt my sin most deeply when Pa led us in nightly prayers. I wondered if God would ever forgive my trespasses against my sister.

We picked our way across Pennsylvania, Ohio, Indiana, and Illinois. The closer we came to Zion, the lighter became our hearts. We were finally approaching our goal, Nauvoo, our heaven on earth.

My bitterness eased as I anticipated learning more of my religion from the lips of the Prophet, Joseph Smith. Perhaps he could teach me a more effective way to petition God for forgiveness.

~ ~ ~ ~ ~

I walked behind our wagon, dusty and footsore, as we approached the outskirts of Nauvoo. The midsummer sun had shone in our faces for hours as it slid down the sky to meet the horizon. John lagged behind me, shielding his eyes with his old floppy hat. My hat was in no better shape than his. I tugged it low over my forehead.

Despite the aches and pains of my weary body, my spirit soared a little higher toward the heavens with each mile gone. We had almost achieved our goal. We had but a mile or two more to travel before we entered the city and joined the Saints in the gathering place.

We began to pass farmsteads, tidy enterprises with crops laid out in patchwork fields. Then we passed a burned-out house, its surrounding fields blackened and nearly bare. I stopped and stared at the view until John drew near.

"That's hard luck," I muttered to my brother. "I wonder if the fields caught first, or if the house fire spread to the crops."

John shrugged, stepped around me, and plodded on toward the wagon. "Come on, Lije," he said. "If I stop, I'll fall over."

I followed him, sorry to see how beaten down he appeared.

After another mile, we passed a tannery, the air redolent with fumes. Next, we came upon a blacksmith shop, where, oddly enough, the anvil was silent. As we approached a cooper's works, with barrels sitting around in all stages of manufacture, I wondered why there were no workers in view. Perhaps the work stopped early on Saturday.

Houses on town lots appeared, large garden patches and

outbuildings to the rear. We had come into the city proper.

"Nauvoo," I whispered to John, unsure if I remembered the correct pronunciation from when our preaching friends had first mentioned the place. That day seemed so long ago, yet here we were at last after a long, troublesome journey. We had reached Zion.

The sun was kissing the earth when we came to a grove of trees that sheltered a large assemblage of people. At the front, his face lit by the dancing light of several torches, a man waved an arm, giving what seemed to be a fiery speech. I couldn't hear the words clearly over the rattle of our wagon, but the air seemed laden with strong emotion.

"Whoa!" Pa reined in our broken-down team, Tom and Bess, and wrapped the lines around the brake handle. The wagon creaked as it settled into repose. Mary Eliza stirred on the seat beside my mother. Ma crooned something to my sister, and she fell silent.

Now I could make out some of the words of the speaker as they rang out in the balmy summer twilight. ". . . have gone to paradise to bear testimony of the wickedness of the world, and help hasten the deliverance of the Saints."

Pa rolled his shoulders, and then leaned toward the sound of the voice.

I walked around the wagon toward the front to stand below my father. A sickening sense of foreboding gathered in my stomach and prickled my spine. I strained to hear the orator.

"It is finished," the man declaimed in the stillness. "It is finished!" he repeated emphatically. "The Saints are free. Jehovah's won the victory, and not a righteous man is lost! Amen."

What could his words mean? A buzz enwrapped the crowd as people shifted at last, engaging their neighbors in hushed tones. Amidst the quiet conversations, I could not pin down the particulars, but I felt the same strong emotion as before. Turning and lifting my face toward my father, I said, "Pa, something's wrong."

He nodded as the speaker led the crowd off toward another section of the town, stragglers lagging behind to grab leftover torches. "It appears you're correct."

Pa vaulted to the ground, and started to follow. As I hastened to catch up to him, I took note that the crowd entered an area that held several headstones. Ahead of the moving assemblage, a group of people, many of them women dressed in black mourning clothing, surrounded what appeared to be open graves. A dreadful feeling filled my bosom.

"Pa!" I cried, and began to run, leaving him behind.

It didn't occur to me that I was a careworn youth, dressed in ragged, dusty clothing, a stranger to this city. All I knew was that something was terribly out of kilter in the world. I heard footsteps pounding behind me. Pa—or John—was following my lead. When I stumbled to a halt on the fringe of the crowd, both of them joined me, and we stood, our breath rasping in our throats, trying to make sense of the gathering.

I pushed my way through the group until I could see the cluster of women standing near the head of the graves. Black veils masked their features. A man wearing a black broadcloth suit stared down at two plain coffins, uttering words intended to comfort the gathering. His halting delivery and tear-streaked cheeks told of his own deep sentiments of grief. He could offer little solace due to his own suffering.

Who were the two souls being consigned to the tender mercies of the Great God of All? My head swam with anxiety. At last, the man in black made the matter clear when he spoke two names: Joseph. Hyrum.

Every Saint knew the names of Joseph and Hyrum. Brothers in the flesh and brothers in the faith. Leaders and prophets and family patriarchs. Joseph Smith, and his elder brother, Hyrum.

I felt a cry gathering in the back of my throat, but before it had more than escaped my lips, a hand clamped over my mouth, and my father led me back through the crowd, tears flooding his eyes. John stood where I had left him, his mouth gaping open.

~ ~ ~ ~ ~

Ma could not believe the Prophet was dead. We had traveled all this distance for the opportunity to sit at his feet and learn, and now he was gone.

"How did it happen?" she asked Pa, but he had no light to shed on the matter yet.

"I will ask, Emily. I will ask."

The huskiness in his voice hurt my soul. For one more night we lay under the stars, camped on the bank of the Mississippi River, listening to the rush of the mighty waters, the crickets and night creatures, and the thuds of our hearts in our chests. We had come here to start again, but never had we imagined such an inauspicious new beginning.

The hurt kept me awake long after my brother's breathing became slow and regular. Brother Joseph was gone. What would become of us, newcomers in Zion? What would become of the Church Joseph had brought forth?

My body hurt as though Hans Stiles had beaten me instead of beating Pa. It hurt as though a wagon had run over me from top to toe. It hurt because my world had toppled around me.

I must have slept at some time during the night, for I opened my eyes to a bright day that seemed at odds with the lack of promise in our situation. We were Saints just as the people in our new locality were Saints, but we were strangers, unknown quantities to our neighbors. And they, just as we, had undergone a terrible loss. Where would the Marshall family fit in?

The question bombarded me throughout the day.

Pa took me with him to find out what had happened and how. We found a people laid low with devastation. No one had foreseen such a calamity when Joseph and Hyrum had surrendered themselves to authorities at the county seat to face charges that had been brought against them. Not even whispers that Joseph had made a morose pronouncement that he "went as a lamb to the slaughter" had prepared them for this occurrence. Yet an armed mob had attacked the jail at Carthage. Joseph and Hyrum had been murdered in cold blood. The fact was inescapable.

Ma wept when Pa told her the circumstances of the death of the prophet and his brother. We all felt sobered, our hope—to hear from his lips the story of the marvelous vision that Brother Joseph had beheld when just a lad—dashed to pieces.

The question on the lips of every person in the city was "Who will lead the Church?" Every mind was confused, every heart gripped with sorrow.

Even so, we found compassion for our situation from the Saints. Although the prophet was dead, the procedure for receiving arriving "converts" such as us, continued to function. Within the first few days of our arrival, we were apportioned a plot of land, a vacant house, seed, chickens, and two half-grown pigs. Pa and I pledged to each work one day in ten on the "temple," a large building on a hill overlooking the city.

Pa decided to plant peas and summer squash, for the growing season was advanced. He reasoned that those crops had the best chance to mature by harvest time. John and I followed him down the designated rows in which he carved holes by hand with a borrowed shovel. John placed three seeds in the earth and I hilled soil on top of them in a manner that would contain water. Mary Eliza was tasked with scooping a ladleful of water from a bucket into the depression of each hill. My job included keeping an eye on her and offering encouragement.

Midway down the row, I turned to see why she wasn't keeping up, then ran back to where she stood, ladling scoop after scoop onto the first mound of the row. "No, Pumpkin. Only one scoop."

She looked up at me, eyes confused.

"This is one," I said, holding up my forefinger. I took the ladle, dipped it into the bucket and moved to the next hill. "One." I demonstrated, then went back and got her to follow me as I advanced to the next place. I scooped. "One here." I stopped myself from saying "too" barely in time. No point in confusing the issue.

From there on, I did double duty, keeping Mary Eliza with me, carrying the bucket, mounding soil over the seeds, then letting her perform her job. I also refilled the bucket from the well when it went dry. Pa and John outstripped our progress by far, but I, bemused by my little sister's prattle, didn't mind keeping her company.

By the end of the day, the patch had been planted and watered, and Ma tucked a tired little Pumpkin—very satisfied with her job well done—into bed.

I sought my own bed with a stretch to relieve sore back muscles, and a sigh. None of us was used to stoop labor, Mary Eliza least of all. However, the girl had acquitted herself well, even when I knew she was tired. Young as she was, she sensed the urgency of getting the crop planted, and the importance of each family member doing their part.

~ ~ ~ ~ ~

Pa took me to the office we had dealt with when we arrived to return the unused seeds and other commodities we could not use. I placed my package on the counter beside Pa's.

The clerk made a note of what we returned, then said, "I hear Samuel Smith is taking charge of the church."

"Samuel Smith, eh. Is he kin to Brother Joseph?" Pa asked.

"His younger brother," answered the clerk. "He's next in line in the Smith family."

Pa nodded, and we left. I was bursting with questions about what would happen next, but knew Pa had no answers to give me. Perhaps we would learn more come Sunday.

Sunday came, and at a quarter to ten o'clock, the family walked to the meeting place, which was a grove of trees with a portable platform set up to accommodate speakers. I felt ill at ease, having attended only two Sabbath services of the faith despite our length of time since baptism. It was, however, a vast relief that we did not have to make over a bar room before the meeting commenced in order to worship God.

Even though we were outdoors, the area was pleasant, a slight breeze playing with the boughs overhead that sheltered us from the sun. Logs and stones indicated where we were to sit. A large number of people were in the process of gathering in the grove. We picked a spot and settled in to find out what would happen in the meeting, and if the church would have a leader soon.

As I looked around, my unease came back. I knew no one here. I missed the small congregation back in Pennsylvania. I missed Paul Peters, with his ready grin and guidance. I even missed his shock of red hair. Unlike Paul, the boys my age took little notice of me. I wondered if the Sacrament of the Lord's Supper would be a part of this meeting. There was no table at the front, and consequently, no cloth covering bread and water or wine.

I still possessed the certificate paper President Peters had given to me after I was ordained a Teacher in the Lesser Priesthood. So far, I didn't know to whom or when I should present it.

At last, several men mounted the steps to the platform.

One arose and gave a number of announcements, and then mentioned that we should expect a call to attend a special conference to be announced later, where common consent of the members would be used to agree or not with Samuel Smith's succession to leadership. This was welcome news. Progress was on the march.

We sang a hymn I didn't know. The prayer of opening that day was far shorter than the one Brother Barnes had given back in Pennsylvania. Then the sermons began.

This time, the other men seated on the stand did not preach. Instead, several other men came when called from the congregation and addressed topics new to me: revelation; saving our dead; and the nature of the Godhead, which I only knew as the Holy Trinity. I was surprised to learn that one of the beliefs to which I now ascribed was that God had a body, a real body similar to my own, and that Jesus Christ was a separate person, with his own body, too. The Holy Ghost, or the Comforter, or a long string of other names, doesn't have a tangible body, but one of spirit only. This, the man told us, was so he could enter into our hearts to do his various jobs. I knew the one about the power to confirm truth to us; Moroni taught that in the Book I had read. I supposed we had felt his comfort during our long winter, else how did we remain positive that we could outlast that trial?

Then the man who opened the meeting rose to finish it off. We sang another unfamiliar hymn, heard a prayer, and left.

That evening, we gathered in our little house for devotions, after which Ma looked toward my brother.

"I have learned that choir practice is held each Thursday night at the Cultural Hall. I think you would like that."

John looked at Pa. "May I go?"

"Most certainly," he said. "You have the gift of song."

Chapter 9

The family worked hard throughout the week, weeding the crops, visiting the sick, and going to various meetings as we got word they were called.

John convinced me to accompany him to choir practice on Thursday night. I was reluctant to go. Over the last two years, my voice had changed to a deeper timbre when I spoke, but I still wasn't sure of it when I sang. Although I had five years of age on him, my brother had no trouble teasing me in all things that made me self-conscious. I certainly didn't want to go out in public and have him sit next to me and poke fun. However, Ma told me to go, so John and I set off for the Masonic Hall, which was also termed the Cultural Hall.

Thankfully, after the choir director had each of us sing a few bars, he assigned us to different sections of the choir.

We practiced several pieces. Some of the singers could read the notes of the music in the hymnal; others couldn't. I had no training, so I was placed between two of my brethren in the "bass" section so I could parrot their musical tones. One held his hymnbook so I could at least see the words to accompany the music we were expected to produce.

I fear I made a bad job of the work, but John's pure tones delighted the director so much that he beamed. In contrast, he frowned when he looked my way. I cringed at his disapproval. I knew I had not my brother's talent. Tonight would most probably be the last time I would bother the director.

The women of the choir sat in front of us, singing praises with great enthusiasm. One young lady turned and stared at me when the director bid us repeat a passage. Had my voice cracked? Was I out of tune? I didn't blush, but I did slip down in my seat as much as I could to escape her notice.

After the practice, the bass singer who had been seated on my left commented on the brightness of the girl's blue eyes, and I learned her name was Amanda Hazelton.

Since he had struck up a conversation with me, I asked if his interests lay in her direction, and he admitted that they did. I wished him good fortune, and decided perhaps the lass had been looking at my neighbor, and not at me. The thought made me feel better, at least. I still had little interest in the fairer sex, as I had no prospects. I also was far too young to commit myself to courtship and marriage. I imagined I would have to be about thirty years of age before I could give much attention to that line of pursuit.

~ ~ ~ ~ ~

The next Sunday as we walked home from services, John made a jest about some trivial mistake I had made during the week, which stung me more than I would have thought over such a minor error. We bantered back and forth until I tired of the matter and fell quiet.

At that point, Ma turned around and addressed John. "Well done, son."

She referred to John's performance with the choir, which sang one of the pieces we had practiced. John, of course, outshone all the other singers. I had not.

John beamed.

I did not.

When Ma had turned back to speak with Pa, I said, "Well

done, son," in a high voice, slapping John on the back, perhaps a bit harder than I would have, had he not seen fit to tease me earlier.

He stumbled a bit from my heavy-handed demonstration of mock praise, then rounded on me and landed a punch on my arm.

The sound of the blow brought my father's eyes upon us, and he was quick to correct our unseemly behavior with a "tsk" of his tongue. We separated by a pace, John lagging behind me as I rubbed the sore spot on my arm.

Not wanting him to get the advantage of me, I turned and began to walk backwards. Unfortunately, my parents and little sister had stopped at a corner to wait for the passing of a carriage. John's wide smile should have warned me, but I missed the significance of his merriment and thudded into my mother, sending her a step or two into the street.

"Emily," my father cried out, and grabbed her arm to pull her to safety.

By this time, I had recovered my balance and turned around, my face going hot from embarrassment and chagrin as I realized Ma had narrowly missed being run down by a passing buggy.

I hung my head, made my apologies in a chastened voice, then let my brother go ahead of me until the right time came to get my revenge.

I saw my chance a little further down the block where several stout sticks lay piled together near our path. I grabbed one up and applied it with vigor to the seat of John's pants. As he howled his protest, I threw it behind me and straightened, adopting an air of innocence.

My incensed sibling turned and launched himself into my midsection, bowling me over onto the grass. As we tussled on the ground, no amount of "tsking" from our father was going to deter John from defending his honor and his seat.

We two went to bed that night without supper, a punishment probably less than we deserved for fighting on the Sabbath day. I surmised that Pa didn't want to break the Sabbath himself by administering well-earned whuppings.

~ ~ ~ ~ ~

It must have been a week later when we got another shock: before he'd had a chance to become the leader of the Saints, Samuel Smith, the Prophet Joseph's brother, suddenly passed from this life.

Sadness and speculation alike took hold in the city. Factions arose, saying this council or that quorum should take the reins of succession. I had no business making a guess as to who was in the right, but I did wonder what was to happen to us all. Our family, in particular, had undergone much tribulation for our faith, not to mention making a grueling journey with played-out horses, a broken-down farm wagon, and scarcely enough food in our bellies to keep a beggar alive. Was it all for naught? I passed through several days of despair before I thought to break open Pa's copy of the Book and read a few passages for consolation.

Then a stir arose with the arrival in Nauvoo of one Brother Sidney Rigdon. A man, passing by on his way home from a Sunday meeting in the grove, gave the news to Pa, who told us that night that because Brother Sidney was the only surviving member of "The First Presidency," he had come to claim what he said was his rightful place of leadership as "Guardian of the Church."

I didn't know Brother Sidney from Adam's off ox, but another bit of news came the next day. President Marks, who I personally did not know, had called a special conference of the Saints of the Nauvoo Stake for August eighth, which date remained a few days off. At the conference, we would be given the opportunity to vote on the matter of accepting Brother Sidney as church guardian, or not.

"We will pray about the matter," Pa said. "We are

entitled to know from God if the thing is right."

I wondered at his words, but duly made my prayers that night a matter of solemn concern. When I rose from my knees and lay on my pallet, I had no answer. I figured God would take his time and give me one through the Holy Ghost when the occasion warranted such a manifestation. That was a bold thought on my part, but it was better than remaining without any hope of settling the question without inquiry to Heaven.

~ ~ ~ ~ ~

The appointed day for the conference arrived. Ma took pains with her grooming and manner of dress, which told me of the importance she gave to the meeting. Had she some secret knowledge to which I was not privy? I thought not, but I had learned that women sometimes have superior talents for inspiration.

Our family arrived at the meeting place and found seats under the spreading limbs of the grove of trees. Many other Saints gathered, some as families, others as single men in small groups of twos or threes. I sat upon a split log next to a young man a few years my senior. The stand before us was occupied by a few men I did not recognize.

Before the meeting began, several men pushed a wagon close by the platform, which seemed to me to be an odd measure, but I didn't know much about the ways of the leaders, so I mentally shrugged and awaited the opening rite.

President Marks called us to order, and then called upon "President Sidney Rigdon" to address us. A man who I supposed was the said Rigdon climbed into the wagon bed, stood up, and spoke for an exceeding long time. I was given by my neighbor on the log to understand that this fellow Rigdon, late of these parts, had been a counselor and confidant of the Prophet, but had moved his household to Pennsylvania some months previous.

Pennsylvania? I had not heard of him from the Saints

when I lived there, but the state spread wide, and I could not claim to know all of its inhabitants.

Mr. Rigdon, having told us at length of a revelation he claimed to have received on the day of the death of the Prophet, continued his discourse by repeatedly telling us that he, having been appointed spokesman to Brother Joseph, was now appointed to be the guardian of the church. He seemed to expect us to accept him in that position straight away.

I didn't feel much sentiment for the man. His manner of speaking was repetitious, and I thought he could have wrapped up his explanation and appeal in twenty minutes.

Sometime after Brother Sidney had been speaking for a while, a well-set man came around the edge of the congregation and took a place on the stand. My log mate dug into my side with his elbow, saying, "That's Brigham Young, back from his mission. Now we'll see a firecracker!"

Mr. Rigdon's oration finally ran its course, and Brother Brigham approached the pulpit on the stand.

We didn't see a firecracker.

In a soft voice filled with pain, Brother Young said he would rather have spent a month mourning his beloved friends, Joseph and Hyrum, than to rise up to do the business of the church so hurriedly.

I turned my head to gauge my father's reaction. Then someone else began to speak words of comfort to us, and I looked toward the stand to see who had taken Brother Brigham's place.

Chapter 10

The same man stood before us and continued speaking in a strangely altered voice. He spoke of the great sorrow he had felt in Boston on the day of martyrdom, without knowing until later of the events that had taken place in the city of Carthage.

I hadn't felt that same sorrow until we arrived in Nauvoo, and wondered if Pa remembered that evil day. I looked again toward him. He gazed with rapt attention at the man behind the pulpit.

A buzz of voices arose in the grove, and my first thought was of censure of the congregation's poor manners. Then I pulled my thoughts up short. Who was I to call anyone to account for their actions? Let Brother Brigham do the job, if he wished.

The sound increased. Pa's eyes widened, and he straightened his posture to bolt upright. What had increased his attention from what I supposed was the fullest concentration possible?

Turning to the front, I beheld an astonishing sight: Brother Brigham had changed in appearance!

I sucked in a raspy breath. Even as my heart began to thump at a furious rate, the murmur of voices again increased in volume. Other members of the congregation saw the same miracle as I did.

I did not know of my own experience whose face Brigham Young now bore, but my heart told me he resembled in countenance, form, and voice, the Prophet Joseph himself. My bosom felt tight, swollen with wonderment.

The occurrence lasted but a fleeting moment and the clamor of voices dropped to an acceptable level when Brigham Young looked and sounded like himself once more. But when he had finished speaking, he speedily dismissed the meeting, asking that the brethren holding the holy priesthood assemble in their quorums at two o'clock here at the stand. The rest of us were to sit in our usual places.

My eyebrows rose. In my experience, when a person went to a church meeting, they remained until all of the business was concluded and the service ended, no matter how long it took. But Brother Young asked us to come to meeting again this afternoon. Perhaps he was put out that he hadn't been the man presiding over this meeting. And yet, he had dismissed it, and no one had protested his doing so.

What was the significance of dividing the higher priesthood holders from the women and children?

I was forced to delay the satisfaction of my curiosity on the matter until later. Possibly, I would also learn the reason for an additional meeting this afternoon. Perhaps I would never know the answers to my questions. Maybe they didn't matter as much as the good feelings I experienced.

I arose, thanked my seat-mate for sharing his information with me, and followed my family out of the grove.

I caught up to them when they stopped to let another family group enter the departing crowd. Pa and Ma were looking at each other, their faces reflecting the puzzlement I felt. Then they both looked at me. My father shrugged his shoulders and made a little "I don't know" movement with his hands, and then we marched away home.

We completed a hasty meal of sliced bread topped with apple butter, and pickles someone had given Ma. They did not hold up to Ma's high standards, but they sat well on my stomach, so I did not question the generosity.

Pa glanced from time to time at his pocket watch, and when he looked up one final time and nodded, I helped carry the tableware and dishes out the back door to the kitchen shed. After Ma set all the dishes and utensils in a basin, I poured hot water over them, and added a bit of the soft soap we used for cleaning up.

Pa's voice came from the house. "Leave the dishes to soak, Emily. I don't want to be late."

I looked at Ma's astonished face. Never before had my father impeded the kitchen work in this manner. I tilted my head, raising my eyebrows in question.

She wiped her hands on a towel. "We'll do as he says, Elijah. This is an important time. The dishes will wait."

~ ~ ~ ~ ~

Back we went to the conference. Pa gathered with other members of the Elders Quorum of the Nauvoo Stake, standing to one side of the platform. Other men stood in other positions around the stand. I was grateful that I had a seat on the grass alongside Ma, John, and Mary Eliza, as thousands upon thousands of Saints crowded into the grove. Word must have spread about the remarkable event that took place during the morning meeting.

A nearly-palpable excitement enwrapped the members. Whispers from earnest voices slowly rose to a crescendo until Brigham Young, a number of men who I later knew to be some of the Twelve Apostles, and President Marks took their places on the stand.

I sat up straight.

The meeting opened in the regular fashion. Brigham Young arose and began to speak, cautioning us to be still, so that all might hear.

I suppose Brother Brigham spoke at least as long as had Sidney Rigdon, but I didn't mind. His subject matter filled my soul, and besides, there was a slim chance that God Almighty would permit us to again see the Prophet Joseph in his person.

We did not receive a further heavenly manifestation, but Brother Brigham called our notice to the fact that for the first time in all our lives, without a prophet at our head, he was stepping forth to act in his calling in connection with the Quorum of the Twelve Apostles. That quorum, he told us, held all the keys of the kingdom of God in the entire world.

He said that when we had the Prophet in our midst, we had walked by sight, without much need to plead to the Lord to know right from wrong. We now were obliged to walk by faith.

I took his point, but since I had never been privileged to sit at the feet of Joseph Smith, I already had done a fair amount of pleading to the Lord. Pa had prayed long and hard to get us through that awful winter of starvation and our heavy losses. I thought I knew what Brother Brigham meant about walking by faith.

He asked us if we wanted a shepherd, a guide, a spokesman to replace the Prophet. I wasn't sure what everything he talked about meant, but when he called for a vote, due to the confusion the question brought to my mind, I didn't raise my hand. Neither did another soul in the congregation.

He asked what we as the people of the kingdom wanted, and then he schooled us on the proper organization of the church. He held up the Twelve Apostles as the proper body to lead the church, because Joseph had blessed them with the keys of the priesthood which he held for eternity. He instructed us that although Sidney Rigdon had claimed it to be so, the man was not on a higher level than the Twelve. Indeed, if the people chose him as leader, it would be up to the Twelve to ordain him to that office, as they alone held the keys of the kingdom.

Although I tried to take in all his words, some of the concepts escaped my understanding. I was obliged to hang on to what I did understand, and yes, to walk by faith.

~ ~ ~ ~ ~

After he had finished his sermonizing, Brother Brigham called upon Brother Sidney to make a rebuttal, but the man replied that he had no more voice, and asked that another brother, W. W. Phelps, speak for him.

Before Brother Phelps could reach the stand, another brother spoke in favor of letting the Twelve remain and act in their place to manage the affairs of the church.

When Brother Phelps took the pulpit, I recognized him as the fiery orator who had preached the funeral sermon of Joseph and Hyrum Smith. I don't know what I expected him to say in support of Brother Rigdon, but my mouth gaped open when he proclaimed, "If you want to do right, uphold the Twelve. I will sustain the Twelve as long as I have breath."

I imagine my surprise was overshadowed by that of Brother Rigdon.

Another elder of the church gave a few remarks, and then Brother Brigham rose for a second speech.

I glanced at the quorums of men, like my father, who had been obliged to stand throughout the speeches. How much longer would they be able to remain on their feet?

Brother Brigham said there was other business to be done, but promised it could be accomplished without calling us all together again.

I sighed in relief as I looked around at the thousands of people spread throughout the meeting ground. *That is wise*, I thought.

He said he would present the leading items, and told us we were to act for ourselves. If we wanted Brother Rigdon, we should vote for him, but not unless we intended to follow and support him.

I'd never thought before on how solemn a thing a vote could be.

Brother Brigham told us the same went for the Twelve. We should not make a covenant to support them, either, unless we would abide by their counsel. He mentioned some other goals the Saints should keep in mind, like finishing the temple as speedily as possible.

I knew we had enemies who would try to prevent us from reaching that goal, and I felt the urgency in Brother Brigham's request.

Then he called upon the quorums surrounding the stand to vote on whether they wanted Brother Rigdon to stand forward as their leader, guide, and spokesman.

Ah. That was why the men of the quorums stood apart from the congregation. Evidently they were to vote as a body of quorum members. I wondered if the rest of us would also be called to do so.

Before the vote could begin, Brother Rigdon got up next to Brother Brigham and whispered to him. Brother Brigham nodded, and then announced, "President Rigdon wants me to bring up the other question first, and that is, does the church want, and is it their only desire to sustain the Twelve as the First Presidency of this people?"

I was ready to vote as Brother Rigdon sat down, but Brother Brigham spoke a bit more before he said, "All that are in favor of this, in all the congregation of the Saints, manifest it by holding up the right hand."

We were clearly being called upon to vote on the issue now. Arms all around me shot skyward, as did mine.

He asked that if there be any of a contrary mind, they were to signify in like manner.

I swept a glance across the immense gathering, but could see no hand in the air. I let out my breath. I didn't know I'd been holding it.

After more remarks, he asked for several votes about

issues such as being tithed until we finished the temple, letting the Twelve teach the bishops how to handle the affairs of the church, and finally, if we would uphold Brother Rigdon in his place in Pittsburgh to build up the kingdom, and to pray for him so that we could have unity.

I voted in the affirmative each time, and saw no contrary votes.

With a final admonition that men stand to their posts and be faithful, Brother Brigham asked Parley Pratt to give a benediction, and then he adjourned the conference for six months.

I sat for a moment, digesting what had occurred. I notice my father shaking hands with several of the elders in his group at the side of the stand, and then he left them and, picking his way through the crowd, came to collect us. Mother rose, holding a sleepy Mary Eliza by the hand, so I got to my feet, nudged John in front of me, and followed them toward home.

~ ~ ~ ~ ~

On our homeward walk, I was struck by the solemnity of my family. Not even Mary Eliza broke the stillness, but she had her thumb in her mouth, so that was to be expected.

My own thoughts turned inward. This morning I had witnessed a miracle. Then the people had voted this afternoon to accept the Twelve Apostles, with Brigham Young at their head, as the rightful leaders of the church. My bosom began to burn and seemed to expand with a confirmation that the plan presented by Brother Brigham was the correct one.

I rubbed my chest. How there was room for my inhalations I did not know, as it surely had already enlarged to its full capacity.

At our house, Pa held the door open and waited until I was about to enter. He kept me outside with a hand on my arm.

"Walk with me," he said.

I did so. We took the path toward the temple on the hill, side by side. An equality of awe surrounded us.

Pa finally spoke, his voice thick with emotion. "This is an exceptional day, Elijah. You may never see its like again."

It took me several more paces before I could reply. "I know it. My body is still . . . buzzing." I wasn't sure that was the most accurate descriptive word, but it seemed right.

"I took note of your attention today."

I didn't know how to reply, so kept silent.

"You are a noble young man."

I threw a quick glance at my father to verify my impression that he was weeping. It was so. My own emotion at the great estimation in which my father held me choked off any response.

"I'm honored that you are my son."

Again, I had no reply. This was high praise from my father. Tears began to course down my cheeks. How fortunate that we soon passed into a thickly sheltered area of the pathway, which served to preserve our dignity.

Pa stopped and turned to me, clapping his hands onto my forearms. He gazed into my eyes. "Lije, always follow Brother Brigham and the Twelve."

I croaked, "Yes Pa. I will."

He released me, turned, and continued toward the temple. I wiped my eyes with the back of my hand and followed after him.

The walls of the temple rose unevenly before us, glittering in the midday sun. Several cranes, which did the work of hoisting stone blocks, stood immobile on this portentous day.

In an attempt to turn my mind from worry about being caught out in the open with tear streaks down my cheeks, I thought about the work I donated to the cause of raising the building. Being neither a stone mason nor a skilled carpenter,

I did odd jobs as requested by whichever foreman directed the labor on my tithing day.

Frequently, I worked at the quarry north of here, which was situated in a dry river bed. Ox teams carried away the rough-hewn limestone blocks. One time, I had been given the task of driving a team from the quarry to the yard where the masons dressed the stone. I fear I had little knowledge of driving oxen, but I did my best. The stone masons did a far superior job. When they had finished with each fine-grained grayish-white block, it resembled marble.

I scrubbed my cheeks with my hands, then, having conquered my emotions and any visible signs thereof, I caught up to my father. He walked along with the sun highlighting his brown hair, which could do with a trim. I brushed my own hair back from where it masked one side of my forehead and tucked it behind my ear. My locks could do with a snipping, too. The sun warmed my back. For today, all was right with my world.

Chapter 11

In the months following the meeting in August, some people left the church. They mainly were those who had not supported Brother Brigham's plan, choosing instead to follow Sidney Rigdon or another of the men who put forth a case for becoming the leader of the church. I didn't pay them much mind, as I was occupied in farming and working on the temple in order that construction could continue at a rapid pace.

A year passed. Pa and I continued our every-tenth-day labors on the temple, as did nearly every man in our stake. A few, who were skilled in construction crafts, worked full time, being paid—if not in cash—with provisions brought into the tithing office.

I'm sure some of our neighbors in the surrounding towns wished we Mormons had disbursed after the deaths of Brother Joseph and Brother Hyrum. Instead, Nauvoo grew with an influx of Saints not only from states east of Illinois, but from across the seas.

A few days before my seventeenth birthday in February, Pa brought home a newspaper. The headline to one article on the front page proclaimed that the Illinois Legislature had voted to strip our city of its legal charter.

As Pa read out the article, I tried to skip ahead by reading to myself over his shoulder.

"That's not fair!" I exclaimed when I saw that we would

lose the right to keep our militia, the Nauvoo Legion.

"Hush, Elijah," Pa said. "Let me read this to your mother."

"The Legion," I muttered. After all the persecution the Saints had undergone in Missouri, I knew the Twelve counted on the militia to safeguard Nauvoo and the church members. My skin crawled, feeling bare, vulnerable. Zion stood in peril.

I gave up reading and went outside to find a chore to take my mind off the bad news. John followed me out.

"What's going on, Lije?" he asked.

I didn't want to frighten him with the notion that our enemies had reached out all the way to the capital in Springfield to put us in dangerous straits again. Hadn't we left such contrivances behind us in Pennsylvania?

Clearly, we had not. Enemies had killed the prophet and his brother. I clicked my tongue. "The city lost its charter," I told him, knowing as I spoke that my answer was unsatisfactory. I picked up an axe and got the whetstone with which to give it a sharp edge.

"Well, what does that mean?" My brother wasn't going to let me off easily.

I sat on a stool in the yard and began to attack the axe head with the stone. "It means the leaders and the Saints don't have the protection we had before. No more Nauvoo Legion to keep us safe."

John's face looked green in the twilight. "That's not good."

"No." I couldn't bear to say more. I had no idea how the Saints would defend themselves from harm.

~ ~ ~ ~ ~

Our disgruntled neighbors, from time to time, painted their faces or wore masks to hide their features when they paid various Saints a visit, trying to persuade them to return to their former places of abode.

One day I was asked to bring a rifle to work with me. After two or three such days on which I acted the part of a guard on my tithing day, I received a summons at the end of my shift. I was to go to the overseer's office. I went right away to see what he wanted.

The overseer sat behind a desk, scribbling in a ledger. When I entered the room, he looked up.

"Brother Elijah, can you be spared at home?"

Taken aback, I almost stuttered my response. "D—do you mean on the farm?"

"Yes. Can your father get by if you are employed here full time?"

"I suppose so, sir." John was helping out regularly, and from time to time Mary Eliza and my mother came out to the field to weed the crop. My labor would be missed, but was not indispensable.

"Good." He selected a cloth sack from a pile on the desk and shoved it and a tin container across the desk toward me. "Report tomorrow to Brother Fleming at the guard post."

I picked up the sack. It weighed a great deal and had an irregular shape. The tin was marked "GUNPOWDER." I picked it up, as well, and tucked it under my arm. "Yes, sir. Thank you sir," I said, took up my rifle, and left the office.

I squatted outside the door and opened the neck of the sack to find it full of lead balls of a size to fit my rifle. No wadding was included. I supposed I would have to provide my own.

Once I arrived at home, I asked Ma for the loan of her scissors, then went to my pallet to find the old shirt I had worn when we arrived in Nauvoo. It was too full of holes to pass down to John, but I had kept it tucked under my bedding, in case I needed it to use as a rag or to cut out a good section for mending another piece of apparel.

I experimented for a while with the cloth and Ma's scissors, and finally found the best diameter of circle to use as wadding when I had to ram a ball down the barrel of my rifle.

Evidently curious at my request to borrow her scissors, Ma came over to me and asked what business I was about. I explained to her about my new employment.

"Elijah! A temple guard? Should I be proud or worried?"

I rose and put my arm around her shoulders, noting that I had grown several inches compared against her height, and now stood taller than she. "I'll let you be proud of me," I said. "There's no reason for concern."

She looked up into my face. "You know there is, else why would you be asked to take this position?"

I squeezed her shoulder. "Nothing in life is certain, Ma."

She sighed. I saw her hand creep onto her stomach. She still mourned the lost babe that the persecution had taken.

"Is not the Kingdom of God worth any sacrifice?" I asked. Even as I spoke the words—and knew them to be true—they sounded glib to my ears in the face of her anxiety.

She nodded, and I wondered how it felt for a parent to lose a child. I grieved for the loss of the tiny brother, but surely not as deeply as did my mother, who had nourished him within her body. Perhaps, one day, if I did not come to any harm guarding the temple, I would have a wife and children. If it pleased God, I would not experience the loss of a child myself.

I shook off the thought, squeezed Ma's shoulder a final time, turned her loose, and resumed cutting patches from my old shirt. It was best that I be well prepared, should the occasion present itself that I be called upon to defend the workmen and the temple.

~ ~ ~ ~ ~

After I let Pa know of my changed availability to work the farm, I began my duties as a temple guard. Sometimes I took my post on the day shift, sometimes at night. I hardly anticipated seeing anything against which I would have to fire my rifle, but it was always at the ready, loaded and primed and slung over my shoulder by a sturdy strap.

One night, I saw a fire a ways off, and my first inclination was to run and help douse it. I might have done so, except that Brother Foster, who guarded another area of the temple grounds, had seen the fire as well. He moved up beside me and placed a hand on my shoulder.

"Be alert, Brother Marshall. The fire may be a diversion."

I hadn't thought of that. I mumbled my thanks for his warning, and went back to my task of walking the west side of the perimeter of the grounds, my stomach muscles clenched. Each rustle in the bushes or snap of a twig drew my attention, and I found myself hunched over protectively, my breathing suspended, listening.

After one such protracted halt in my progress, I straightened up and rolled my shoulders, trying to work out the stress building in my muscles. I could still see the fire, but several minutes before, men had arrived to put it out. I had just reached for my canteen to take a sip of water when I heard gunfire.

After I beat down my alarm, I realized it was not close by, nor aimed my way, but rather came from another section of the city. From my vantage point on the prominence, I watched muzzle flares originating from two opposing spots. I yearned to join in the defense of a fellow Saint's property, but was constrained by my employment as temple guard.

How I managed to uproot my feet and make my rounds as the fight continued, I do not know. What I did was continue to halt and listen to any slight disruption in the sounds around me.

Several men joined in the fight below. They drove off the attackers, whoever they had been, and gradually, peace descended on the city again. I kept to my duties even though my stomach clenched anew at every sound for the rest of my watch.

On Sunday, I joined a group of young men standing

around waiting for our church meeting to begin, and learned that a small group of masked men had come into the city by night during the week and set fire to a barn. No one knew if they were the same men responsible for the gun shots fired at a group of Saints going home from a council meeting. I felt the same tightening in my gut as I had on the night of the activity, and hoped Ma would not hear of these events.

~ ~ ~ ~ ~

Several more times, unknown men came into the city and caused a ruckus in the hours of darkness. Then I moved to the day shift for two weeks, and heard no more about masked interlopers.

When my turn came again to take the night shift, Ma hugged me fiercely and commanded me to be careful. That's when I learned that my mother was aware of the incidents.

The first night was uneventful. So too, was the second. On the third, a volley of shots, some aimed in my direction, broke the quiet of nighttime.

I took cover behind a block of limestone left on the ground for tomorrow's workmen to lift onto the wall, and unslung my rifle. My hands shook. What was I supposed to do? No one had given me instruction as to how to proceed if the temple were to come under attack. Remembering the fire I had witnessed, I wondered if these men had come to burn the temple.

I peered over the block and noted the muzzle blasts from two weapons. Ducking down, I got my rifle in a satisfactory position, counted to myself, one, two, three, then rose up and fired toward the place where I had seen one discharge. I didn't let myself wonder if I had hit anyone, but ducked again and busied my mind and hands with reloading. Then I pushed myself to the other end of the stone before taking a look at my opponents' line. No one was firing just then, and I worried that they had jumped the fence and were moving toward me. I dared not call aloud to the other guards. Surely they had come to repel the invaders, but what if they had not? I had to suppose myself alone in the defense of the temple.

Wishing I didn't have to waste lead and gunpowder—not to mention my patches—I began to lay down as quick a fire as I could muster toward random spots along the fence line. Although I'd never practiced fast reloading for defensive purposes, a healthy dose of fear helped me quicken my movements.

At last I heard shots from other points along the temple wall. I hoped they came from friend, not foe, but couldn't take the time to speculate for long. Instead, I kept up my fire.

The moon rose, and shortly thereafter, I heard the beat of multiple horses' hooves, starting at the area of the fence and receding toward the edge of the city. Were the men leaving due to the threat of discovery in the moonlight? I held my breath to listen. Nothing stirred in the direction of the fence. I sank down behind the stone and breathed again, my head tilted back to draw in fresh air.

"Marshall?"

"I'm here," I called, then moved, in case someone had been left behind to watch and snipe.

Names rang out, with corresponding answers from the other guards. One of our braver men came from the direction of the fence, calling softly, "They've cleared out, but I found blood."

Of course we all trooped down to see. Had I wounded someone, a man bent upon doing me harm?

Brother Foster held up a length of calico with holes cut into it, probably as a mask. A dark area marked where it was soaked with blood. "Someone bandaged a wound," he said. "It must have fallen off when they fled."

We walked the fence on the outside, finding burnt wadding here and there, but nothing that would identify the marauders. Once our outrage had dissipated, we each went back to our posts, and spent the rest of our watch in uneventful, if cautious, peace.

Chapter 12

The Twelve Apostles called the Saints to come to a conference in October, my third such general gathering of church members since our arrival in Nauvoo. This conference would be different in one respect: it was to be held within the walls of the temple instead of out in the grove.

The Brethren also issued an invitation to attend a special meeting on the first Sunday morning of the month to dedicate the temple. If we could get inside, we could attend.

Sunday came. We'd had a hard frost overnight. The leaves on our trees had begun to turn yellow. Withered grass sparkled with ice crystals as I tended to the animals before breakfast.

Ma hurried Mary Eliza along with eating her breakfast so we would have a chance to get into the meeting, but her dawdling almost cost us that opportunity. When we arrived on the temple block, many other Saints were there before us. We only managed to enter at the last minute and had to stand at the back, in front of the choir gallery.

Brigham Young opened the meeting with a prayer of dedication, in which he presented the temple, as much as was completed, to the Lord, as a monument of the Saints. He prayed, "Lord, we dedicate this house and ourselves, to thee."

A shiver ran through me. The head of the church had given me over to God.

Several other speakers followed Brother Brigham. They all bore their testimonies, giving us instruction and teachings pertaining to this auspicious occasion.

As the meeting wound down, the men of the city were instructed to reassemble at two o'clock. When we took our leave, I wondered if I was counted a man yet, but as it turned out, Pa didn't invite me along when he left for that appointment.

I wasn't sure how put out I was. In a few short months, I would be eighteen years old. Just last month I'd been selected to be a temple guard. Didn't that count for something?

I spent the time before Pa came back sighing and trying to focus on my perusal of Pa's Book of Mormon. Ma kept giving me the eye. I figured she was disgusted with me, and she had every reason to be. How would anyone think I was a man when I still fell into such childish fits of pique?

When Pa came home from that three-hour meeting, he spoke quietly to Ma, but would not divulge the details to the rest of us.

"Pay attention tomorrow, Lije. Perhaps you'll learn what I learned today."

With that, I had to be satisfied.

~ ~ ~ ~ ~

Monday was ordinarily a work day, but we put on our Sunday-best clothes and gathered at the temple. It took a long time for everyone to arrive and take their seats, but at last the meeting convened.

Brother Brigham presided, flanked by five other members of the Twelve Apostles and the presidency of the Nauvoo Stake. A choir, which occupied the gallery at the rear, sang to open the proceedings. John's clear voice would have been a good addition to the singers, but he had not been invited to participate.

Brother Pratt offered a prayer. Elder Richards was the first speaker, and he started off scolding us for our lack of punctuality, noting that President Young had waited from nine-thirty a.m. until almost eleven for us to gather. He encouraged us to be more prompt in arriving henceforth, as there was much important business to address during the conference. I felt suitably chastised, although our family had been on time.

Our stake president, Uncle John Smith, as he was called, was asked to present the authorities of the church for a sustaining vote. I thought we had taken care of this matter in August, when Sidney Rigdon had made his play, but evidently we were to repeat it in each general church conference, so I held my arm crooked at the level of my chest so I could raise it quickly and have done with it.

Make no mistake, I was happy to give my support to our church leaders, but I was impatient to know what Pa wouldn't divulge yesterday.

President Smith spoke out the names of each of the Twelve Apostles as Presidents of the whole church. I had expected to sustain them as a body, but such was not the case. We were to vote on each one individually. To my surprise, some men raised objections to a couple of the members of the quorum. In the first instance, the Prophet Joseph's younger brother, William Smith, lost his place, but the case of another apostle, whose whereabouts were presently unknown, was held over until he could be located. Having done his duty, President Smith sat down.

One of his counselors, Brother Isaac Morley, arose and presented the name of William Smith again, but this time as the Patriarch of the church. After all this time, I still didn't know what a patriarch did for the church, but Brother William must have been found in grave errors, because he also lost that position. When Brother Morley sat, I wondered if the office would be vacant for long.

President Young, as I now meant to think of him, presented other names for us to approve. My head began to swim as I tried to keep all the leaders straight. Maybe an account would be published in the *Nauvoo Neighbor* or the *Times and Seasons*, and I would be able to make more sense of it all. One thing did catch my notice. President Young proposed that a quorum of Deacons be selected. I surmised that this was something new, and readily raised my hand to sustain the action. Perhaps I would be invited to be a part of that quorum. Then I remembered the certificate paper President Peters had given me after my ordination said I was a Teacher. I still hadn't been asked to perform any duties of the office, and wondered, in our unsettled circumstances, when I ever should.

By now, President Young had concluded his business and called for another meeting to commence at two o'clock p.m., after which the current session was adjourned.

~ ~ ~ ~ ~

I walked home somewhat sobered, and thoroughly disappointed. Perhaps we would have had more meaty matters presented to us if the meeting had taken up on time. I wondered what the afternoon assembly would bring.

Notwithstanding my lack of appreciation of the business that had taken place, one thought gave me pause. One member of the Prophet's family had lost his way in error. Another, his paternal uncle, continued steadfast. Since I didn't understand all that had gone on in the meeting, did I have the proper foundation to remain steadfast myself?

Sarah hadn't.

I missed that sister of mine, head turned by a scalawag. Where was she? Was she in good health? Would I ever see her again? I mourned for a good part of my walk home, wondering if I would follow Sarah's example and lose my way like William Smith had.

Then I remembered the words of President Young last August. He said we now were obliged to walk by faith, instead of seeing everything firsthand. I had to trust in God's loving kindness, and go forth to perform my duty, if ever I discovered what *that* was.

My thoughts wandered from duty to members of my extended family. Where had *my* paternal uncle, John Marshall, taken his family when he parted from my father to homestead a new farm? Was he near enough to learn of Sarah, to take care of her if she were in dire straits? I just did not know.

My brother had been named for Uncle John, while I was given the name of my grandfather on my mother's side, Elijah Scow. From time to time I had thought on my mother's older sisters, my aunts, who had married and scattered to the four winds, leaving my mother, the youngest sibling, to stay at home until my father came along to woo and win her. My parents had moved onto the ancestral farm when Uncle John decided to seek new land, but I didn't know where my uncle's family had ended their journey.

My ruminations caused me to realize that family was precious to me, but with so much persecution about, we were hard pressed to defend ourselves. Trying to reestablish contact with our kin at this time was out of the question.

~ ~ ~ ~ ~

In the afternoon, Elder Parley P. Pratt gave the first address. He discussed why the Saints were building houses and a temple when they planned to leave the city in the spring.

His words struck me as though by lightning. I had heard rumors that the mobs wished to drive us out of Nauvoo, but not that the church leaders would give in to their demands.

"The people of God always were required to make sacrifices," he continued.

Yes, that was true, if my reading of the Old Testament was any measure.

"If we have a sacrifice to make," Brother Pratt said, it should be something worthy of the people of God. Nauvoo was to be left as a monument to the people.

That sounded familiar. President Young had said as much about the temple. Why hadn't I caught the underlying meaning of his address that day—that we would leave Nauvoo behind?

Brother Pratt said, "The people must enlarge in numbers and extend their borders. They cannot always live in one city, nor in one county." He concluded with a reminder that ancient prophets had foretold the destiny of the Saints of the last days.

He was saying we would become a mighty people! I could hardly fathom the thought, having become accustomed to most of the Saints living together in one area, but there were Saints in the Eastern states, and even many overseas. It made sense that we had to move. We would need a place where there was room to expand, a place with land enough for all. I still worried about how we, the Marshall family, would acquire the goods and supplies we needed.

President Young arose. His address was powerful and yet encouraging. He spoke of the task awaiting the leaders of moving all the Saints out of Nauvoo, but added, "If you will be faithful to your covenant, I will now prophesy that the great God will shower down means upon this people, to accomplish it."

I felt a surge of emotion swell my bosom, and glanced over at Pa. He was gazing into Ma's eyes, holding her hand, and as I looked on, he squeezed it firmly. I looked away.

Then we were asked to vote whether we as a church would move en masse from the United States, with all its persecution, and go to a country far to the west where we could serve God unmolested by mobs.

The vote was unanimous.

~ ~ ~ ~ ~

The Conference continued on Tuesday, with exhortations to be unified and willing to leave everything behind, even if property could not be sold. Elder Heber C. Kimball boldly stated that he would prophesy in his own name that within five years, the Saints would be as well off as they were now.

When the second meeting began at two p.m., there was a bit of excitement when President Young came to the stand and dismissed the meeting until the next day because a body of armed men had suddenly entered the city. He enjoined the brethren to go to their homes and prepare for any emergency.

By the time Wednesday came, the turmoil had passed, and we spent another day of counsel and encouragement divided into two sessions.

To open the afternoon session, the choir sang a stirring number entitled "The Spirit of God Like a Fire is Burning," which tightened my throat with emotion. Elder Taylor discussed the matter of discontinuing publication of the two city newspapers. To my relief, the conference minutes were to be published first. By reading them, I could learn the facts of who held which office, which my wretched brain had not retained. I hoped to increase my knowledge of the church's leadership thereby.

Elder Kimball gave a stern admonition not to shoot our neighbors' cattle that wandered into our fields and did damage to our gardens. This must have been a serious problem, for although we had suffered no such loss, nor blazed away at any neighbors' cows, a proposal was made that any found guilty of this crime would be cut off from the church unless they made restitution.

With a few other sober pronouncements, the conference was adjourned until the following April. I expect I had learned what Pa referred to: our people were to leave Nauvoo the following spring, and we had a lot of work before us.

Chapter 13

Persecution increased over the next weeks. Each day I left for my employment, haunted by the look in my mother's eyes as she patted my shoulder and bid me farewell. I could not know if, indeed, that was to be our final farewell. Would harm come to me at the temple lot? To my family during my absence? I developed a knot of dread in my innards that never really untied from day to day.

After it became apparent that I was needed at home to harvest our crop as well as to prepare for our departure, I asked to be released from my full-time employment as a temple guard, and permission was granted, although I still performed that duty on my tithing days.

Pa and I began to work on the old wagon in which we had traveled from Pennsylvania. When the ordinary farm chores had been finished for the day, we engaged ourselves in replacing nearly every plank and fitting on the vehicle by lamplight. On some days, he and John did the chores and I worked on the wagon, following his specifications. On other days, John and I did the chores while Pa labored on the wagon.

Our days of toil slipped away. I fretted that perhaps we wouldn't finish the work on the wagon—but also on gathering supplies—before the day of departure arrived. I fretted that our enemies might overrun us before the temple had been completed.

Pa must have had enough of my worrisome attitude. "All will be well, Lije," he said. His familiar theme of comfort seemed at odds with the gravity of the situation, but his words did sooth a few of my fears.

As fulfillment of his faith, we reaped a bounteous harvest of our crop, which we peddled in surrounding towns on a neighbor's borrowed farm wagon. With the proceeds, we were able to lay in stores of flour, sugar, and other foodstuffs. Pa and I did manage to finish work on the wagon, and he purchased two yoke of oxen to pull it. He judged that the horses were now too old and worn down, and unsuited for the task ahead.

Winter arrived. With harvest completed, I was again employed as a temple guard. It seemed not a night passed without a fire or other commotion raising an alarm in the city, or a day when refugees from the outskirts came into town, reporting their farms destroyed and their family members threatened, or worse.

In mid-December, under the direction of Brother Brigham, the apostles began to hold special gatherings in the attic story of the temple, which had been dedicated for the purpose of extending special blessings to the Saints. Those who were elders in the priesthood were invited to bring their wives and come to receive their endowment of such blessings.

I had not achieved sufficient age to become an elder, so I did not attend a temple meeting to receive an endowment. However, my parents went to one of the day-long sessions.

When they returned home that evening, I felt a change, a peace emanating from their persons. In Pa, it seemed to magnify the same steady faith that had guided his life since the elders had visited our farm. That day in the temple, however, gave Ma more peace and serenity than she had possessed for a very long time.

I wondered what had occurred that had changed Ma's outlook, but by now I knew better than to ask about things reserved for me to learn at another time.

~ ~ ~ ~ ~

Marauders burned farmsteads and homes on a regular schedule in the new year of Our Lord, eighteen forty-six. Newspapers in other towns in Hancock County harangued the Saints with all manner of falsehoods. Brother Brigham and eight other apostles had an indictment filed against them. Who accused them of counterfeiting, I do not know, but the threat to our leaders of becoming incarcerated pressed down upon our hearts. Everywhere I went, people spoke of how Brother Joseph and Brother Hyrum were murdered while in Carthage Jail. No one could bear to think of losing much of our church leadership to death again.

We soon heard of a message sent by Governor Ford, saying that federal troops from St. Louis would hunt down the Saints and destroy them. With every hand against us, it was time to go, time to leave our homes behind and launch ourselves on a journey to the west. My heavy heart protested against the fact that we had to leave Zion.

Brother Charles Shumway led out in early February—a miserable, cold day—to wait for the ferry to dodge drifting ice floes in the river so it could cross to the Illinois side to load his wagon. I gave up counting the rickety wagons creaking past to join the exodus down Parley Street to the ferry landing after I reached two hundred. John kept up the count, though, and reckoned that more than five hundred families had waited in line by mid-month.

We finally settled up our debts by selling our holdings in Nauvoo for pennies on the dollar to a man from Quincy, who told Pa that he wanted us off his lot by the end of the next week.

Accordingly, we packed the wagon, hitched up the oxen, and tied Tom and Bess behind, for although they could not pull the wagon, we would use them to pack Ma's rocking chair, her churn, and other such sundries as she could not bear to leave behind. Ma swept out the rooms and put the broom behind the door. Then we got into line and waited our turn to cross the Mississippi.

On the western shore, we topped a prominence in a driving rainstorm. I looked across the river to our lost Zion, and gazed at the temple that I had worked upon and defended. I heard Ma sniffling behind me. I gave her time to compose herself, then turned to find her caught in Pa's embrace. I looked aside as I strode past them, unwilling to intrude on their raw grief. Mary Eliza sobbed openly in the wagon. John shrugged when I asked him how he fared. I patted his shoulder, then got the oxen underway so we could find a place to camp.

We rested that night at a place called Sugar Creek, taking shelter from a sleet storm under a canvas tent that needed waterproofing in the corners that somehow escaped my applications of wax or tallow.

It chafed me a bit not to know where we were bound. Where was Zion to be found? Were we journeying to Oregon, to Vancouver Island, as had been noised about, or to California? I knew our destination was not Texas, despite the pleas of several explorers who last year had been cut off from their membership when they would not heed the counsel of the Brethren to return to the body of the Saints. As I ate supper, I put away my worries. Well, nearly all of them. One stuck in my mind: Why wasn't I more like Pa, whose trust in the Brethren was infinite?

I slept that night under the wagon, and awoke to a cocoon of snow surrounding our cramped place in the camp.

~ ~ ~ ~ ~

"Hell's bells!"

I'd never heard my mother curse before, and even that mild expletive coming from her lips shocked me as I sat on my somewhat soggy blankets and pulled on my boots.

"Emily," my father cautioned. "Mary Eliza—"

"Have you ever tried to coax a fire to life in a snowbank?" Ma's tone was colder than the weather.

Indeed, snow covered the ground in great heaps. I could see the difficulty in my parent's task, but she must be truly exhausted to have succumbed to using that language.

I went to help her, and found myself warming up from the labor of scraping snow aside to find bare ground, which offered a much improved prospect for a roaring fire.

A roaring fire was exactly what we needed as the temperature dipped lower throughout the day. I ranged wide from the camp to find firewood. I met many others engaged in the same pursuit, and when we did find a wooded slope, how our axes rang in the still air!

Five of us fashioned a rude sled and laid our logs upon it for the dash back to camp, hauling it in turns until we got the prize back to our individual firesides.

When I had chopped enough fuel for the fire—my body immediately cooling after I stopped my labor—I was obliged to huddle with the family near the fire, enduring a wind-driven smoke. The cold crept into my bones whenever I got up to move about, and I imagined it was worse for my parents, given their somewhat advanced age.

We endured inclement weather for several days, while a stiff wind blew to make us even more miserable. In the meantime, Brother Brigham and the apostles set about formulating rules for behavior in our camps, and a schedule to follow as we moved west.

~ ~ ~ ~ ~

We finally got the word to move on. We traveled with some difficulty for several days, crossing a river on a submerged ledge of rock, then camped at a place called Richardson's Point.

Pa and I learned that we would be here for ten days or more, so we went out into the country, seeking work. Pa found a place with a crew building a house, but I had to travel on down the road a piece until a farmer put me to work husking corn.

Back in camp, Ma used John to haul water so she could do laundry. She took the occasion to school Mary Eliza in the household arts she previously had not been old enough to learn.

Surprisingly, my farmer paid me cash money for my labors. When Pa and I pooled our earnings, we had enough money to buy a few supplies that we had lacked up to now.

Again we traveled on, but spring storms, fiercely cold, overtook us, and we only traveled for a few days in rain and snow before we came to another river, this one with steep, moisture-slicked banks.

Pa peered down into the gulf. "We'll have to double-team the wagons, Lije. Let's go find out the plan."

I'd never been as tired and sore before as I was by the end of that day. Pa and I—and sometimes John—hitched extra oxen to one wagon after another, drove them down the bank, up the other side, and then returned to the eastern bank to do it all again. I fell asleep during the nightly prayers, and Ma had to shake me vigorously before she roused me enough that I could stumble to my bedroll.

Chariton Camp became another waypoint. Many of the Saints had come down with colds, chills, or fever, and no one hoped to travel on in that condition. I was one of those so afflicted, to my shame. I coughed until I thought my insides would change places with my outsides. Ma was obliged to mix a mustard plaster to apply to my chest. I wasn't sure which was worse—the cough, or the burn to my skin from the crushed mustard seeds. Gradually, with some days of rest, my health improved.

President Young took the occasion of our layover to reorganize the four hundred or so wagons in the company into groups of fifty, with even smaller groups of ten wagons. Our family learned we had been transferred from one group to another. I wasn't sure what effect that would have on us. It didn't change the weather.

We traveled on, stopping from time to time, hopping across the prairie in fits and starts as the weather and conditions of the roads dictated. Despite the mud, by mid-April trees began to leaf out, and grass sprouted, spreading a carpet of green that excited our teams of oxen. Pa and I became quite proficient at snapping a bullwhip above their heads to encourage them to move forward instead of stopping to graze.

With only a week lacking until the end of the month, we halted again at a place on the headwaters of the Weldon Fork. This spot, christened Garden Grove, was designated as a temporary settlement. Although we were not going to stay here, Pa, John, and I were assigned to work details, spreading out to dig a well, fell trees for cabins, and herd flocks. Other men split rails for fences, fashioned handles for plowshares, and built a bridge.

One night after supper, a man camped nearby brought out his fiddle and another joined him with a guitar, and we commenced to dance to the lively music they produced. Ma pulled me into a circle dance, then came a reel, and several country dances followed. By this time, Ma had abandoned me in favor of dancing with Pa, and I was left to my own devices. I found that a nicely-put-together young lady had paused beside me, clapping her hands and tossing her head, so I bucked up my courage, turned to her, and proposed that she join me in making merry. She laughed and agreed, and we had an entertaining evening.

Chapter 14

I wasn't keeping close track of time, but I believe it was late in the month of May when we topped a rise and saw before us a wayside camp. What a prospect greeted us! The Saints who had arrived before us had built a settlement. Half-built log cabins and tents occupied one section, while another, larger section was under the plow in preparation of planting a crop. Through this rough community ran the muddy road to points west, which I fully expected us to follow in a day or two. As we descended, I could see that several families dwelt in caves dug into the hillside.

Once we parked our wagon, I went with Pa to find whoever had charge of the place, in case we should be obliged to abide by any particular regulations in setting up camp. Directed to a Brother Hunt, we found him in one of the unfinished cabins.

"Welcome to Mount Pisgah, brethren," he greeted us, ushering us behind a curtain to an area outfitted as an office, with a small camp desk off to one side, and various stores of supplies piled about the remainder of the spot. "Now then," he said, sitting himself on a stool behind the desk, "have a seat." He opened a green-bound book, which proved to be a ledger of some sort, dipped a steel-nibbed pen into a bottle of ink, and looked at us.

Pa had taken a straight-backed chair. I looked around for

another accommodation, and seeing that my choices were a box or a barrel, I remained on my feet.

"Name?" Brother Hunt asked.

"James Marshall. This is my son, Elijah."

The man wrote out our names. "Have you a wife?"

"Mrs. Emily Marshall," Pa said. "Two other children besides, John and Mary Eliza."

Brother Hunt dipped the pen several times as he wrote our names in his book. He looked at me, probably decided I didn't have the age to be married, then addressed my father again. "Occupation?"

"Farmer, although I've done my share of rough carpentry," Pa replied. "We both worked on the temple." He jerked his head toward me. "Elijah held a post as temple guard."

"Hmm," said the man, looking at me with eyebrows raised, then wrote it all down. When he had finished, he tapped the shank of his pen against his lips for a moment, then asked Pa, "Have you a plow in your wagon?"

I looked at Pa, and he looked at me. Then he turned back to Brother Hunt. "We do."

The man put down his pen, steepled his fingers, and peered at Pa. "Would you consider staying a few months to put in a crop of buckwheat and get it on its way before you continue west?"

"Do you mean for us to stay until harvest time?"

"No, only until mid-summer or so. Then you may follow Brother Brigham to the Missouri River."

"Who will harvest the crop?"

"The Saints who will come behind you." Brother Hunt leaned back on his stool and pursed his lips.

Pa considered for several moments with his head slightly bowed. I wondered if he was praying about the matter, or considering what Ma would say about staying here for a while. After what seemed like an hour, he slowly nodded his head. "We will do it."

This response took me by surprise. Pa had wanted so badly to press forward alongside the leaders to the Missouri. Perhaps he was more worn down than I had supposed, and needed a rest from the hard labor of travel. Not that farming was effortless, but staying a few months in Mount Pisgah might afford us a welcome change.

Brother Hunt rose and leaned over his desk, extending his hand to Pa. "That is good," he said, pumping their clasped hands up and down. "We can use your help." Sitting down again, he asked, "Have you a tent?"

Pa nodded.

"Pitch it at the end of this row, and I'll put you on the list for getting a cabin built." He looked in his ledger. "Three children, correct?"

Again Pa nodded.

"Then you'll want twelve-foot sides." He turned several leaves of the book and made an entry.

I should not have been surprised at his efficiency. Notwithstanding it being a brand new camp, order seemed to be the hallmark of this settlement, as was the case in the others we had stopped at over the months of our journey. Brother Brigham and the apostles had done a good job of planning for our migration, but the weather impeded our passage across the territory of Iowa. Delays come from the heavy rains and resultant mud. No one could have planned perfectly in the face of nature's obstacles.

Brother Hunt closed the ledger and looked up. "In a few days, we'll raise your cabin, not more than a week, I'm sure."

Pa stood. "Thank you, brother. Come, Lije."

~ ~ ~ ~ ~

Until Pa could round up men to help us build a cabin from logs, we lived in a tent. Ma made the acquaintance of a Sister Eliza Snow, who, having just done the same to her own cabin, advised Ma that once the walls were up, she should have the workers spread our tent cloth over the ridge pole and fasten it down tight on two sides. A week later, men assembled to put up the walls of our new abode. Pa took the woman's advice, and our home served us well with the canvas roof for a time, until we put on a proper shake roof.

Pa, John, and I engaged ourselves in plowing up a good-sized parcel of land to put in the buckwheat, as requested. Pa gave John the task of drawing water for each day's needs out of a slow-moving brook close by the settlement.

Ma took Mary Eliza with her to visit a woman who had given birth to the first child in the settlement, a Sister Pratt. They learned that the woman's husband, Parley, who was one of the Apostles in the Twelve, had been the one who named the place Mount Pisgah. He thought he could see the Promised Land—as did Moses of old—when he topped the eastern hill. It was a charming story, but I was just as glad for the evening meal that night as I was for the news.

The next day while working in the field, I had an episode of what would be called "scours," were I a calf. The condition reoccurred throughout the day, but passed through me by nightfall. When it happened again a few days later, I tried to determine what element of my diet might have caused the debility. After sorting out in my mind the meals I'd consumed over the course of the past week, I realized Ma had served nothing unusual. The only variance was in the water hauled by John. I thought it tasted odd from day to day.

I approached him about the subject that night.

"John, where are you dipping the water buckets?"

He looked at me like I'd grown a second head, but gave me an answer. "Out of the pool by the stunted oak. You know, the one with the lightning slash on one side."

I grunted in reply. I knew the place. The fallen top of the oak had dammed up most of the water's flow to create a perfect pool for getting water. Unfortunately, I'd seen men relieving themselves there, leaning one hand against the oak's trunk until they had finished their business.

"How about you go upstream from there a ways?"

"That's the best spot."

"I don't think so." I had tasted urine in the water I drank with supper. "I prefer free-flowing water. Walking a few yards upstream to get it won't harm you."

"Those buckets are heavy, Lije. If you want to trade chores and do it yourself—"

"No," I cut him off. "Just take care in where you draw the water. It tasted foul tonight."

"Tasted fine to me."

I made a face as though I were gagging. "That's where folks pee," I whispered so Ma wouldn't hear me.

"Yuck," John said. "Why didn't you tell me before this?"

"I thought you'd taken notice," I said. "Go upstream some before you dip your buckets."

John agreed, and that was that.

For about two weeks after that, my bowels behaved themselves, but after another stint of scours, I discovered that John had become lazy, and was again drawing water from beside the lightning-blasted oak.

"I was sick today," I told him after supper. "You're not heeding what I said."

He hung his head in acknowledgement of the error of his ways. "The buckets are heavy," he gave as an excuse, then added, "I was also sick some today. Do you reckon it's the water?"

"That's all I can make it to be. You've got to be more careful."

"I'm sorry, Lije. I'll do better."

I let him go off to bed, but wondered if I should ask Ma to boil the water. She and Pa hadn't come back from an after-supper visit with a new family, though, and the next day, I forgot about my contemplated request.

On several occasions, Pa and Ma visited newcomers after

we had eaten supper, mostly to see if any of them were former neighbors from Nauvoo. One night, they came through the door, talking animatedly. I noticed that Ma wore a handkerchief over her nose and mouth, which I thought curious.

Pa called for prayers so that we could retire to bed. His prayer that night included a call for blessings upon those who were sick of the cholera.

A chill ran down my spine, for I knew cholera was a serious ailment that could result in death. I hoped Pa and Ma had not put themselves in harm's way.

~ ~ ~ ~ ~

A couple of weeks later I was asked to go out with a party of young men to cut and haul logs for more cabins. I rose before the sun was up, grabbed a baked potato and a boiled egg for breakfast and filled my canteen, then set off with the men on our journey to the hills to the north.

We tarried several days, cutting logs to raise cabins for several more families, then got our load together and returned to the settlement. I marked it as strange that I didn't see my father or brother cultivating the buckwheat fields as we passed.

I pitched in to unload the logs. A brother from the settlement came to help us. Upon seeing me, his countenance took on a pale color and his limbs began to shake in the most astounding manner. After a few moments, he recovered himself and stammered something about me being needed at home.

Feeling uneasy, I asked leave of the job foreman to go see what family disaster had caused the man to react in such a way. I was dismissed, and making as much haste as I could without actually running through the streets, arrived at the cabin that served as our home in Mount Pisgah.

The front door opened. A woman came out, saw me, and caught her breath in such a distressed manner that I immediately petitioned her to tell me what mischance was afoot.

"Oh Elijah," she said, and began to weep.

I pushed past her, alarmed at this second indication of a dire occurrence. I found my family abed, except for Mary Eliza, who stood with her back against the log wall, whimpering and wiping her eyes with her rumpled apron. Several women stood around my parent's bed, whispering something I didn't catch, but I could see nothing of my mother and father. I looked toward the cot I shared with my brother. A sheet of cloth entirely covered an unmoving form.

I cried aloud, "John," and flung myself in that direction. Someone caught my arm, but I shrugged free of the clutching hand and swept the cloth aside. My brother lay with his hands crossed upon his breast. "No!" I shouted, kneeling and cradling his head in my embrace. "No."

I couldn't breathe. My fingers splayed backwards, stiff as twigs. John couldn't possibly be dead. He only slept deeply, as he was wont to do.

"John," I commanded. "Stop playing around. Your joke isn't funny."

He didn't stir, didn't open his eyes and shriek, "Boo!" I put a fingertip underneath his nose, wanting with all the power within me to feel the moist whisper of his breath. There was none.

No, no, no.

A woman grasped my arm, trying to raise me up as she said, "You must bid your parents farewell."

Farewell? My mind reeled. What great calamity was this? I laid down my brother's lifeless head, pushed myself upright, and followed the sister toward the group surrounding the other bed.

As though by magic, the way parted. I finally heard what the sisters were murmuring. *Cholera.* I cast my eyes upon my dam and sire engaged in breathing their last.

"Mother," I cried out. She opened her eyes a bit, seemed to recognize me, and as I bent toward her, she strained to whisper, "Take care of your sister."

"I will."

That was her last communication, laying upon me a great charge. I felt as though my heart had ceased beating. My mother was gone. How was I to care for Mary Eliza alone?

"Come," said another woman, and led me to the side of my father.

His breathing was as shallow as I had ever seen, but he, too, struggled to leave me a message. I took his hand and knelt at his side, and he murmured, "Follow the leaders to Zion." Then his hand lost all life, and I was an orphan.

I was an orphan, and brotherless, with a small sister who still huddled against the wall of our primitive home.

I sobbed.

I cried with a heart so heavy I thought it would sink out of my body and straight through the floor. I have no idea how long I carried on, bleating like a frightened lamb, until I recalled that such sounds must be causing Mary Eliza a terrible alarm. It was all I could do to get myself together, wipe my eyes, and go to her where she crouched in the corner.

I sat on the floor beside her and pulled her against my chest. She began to sob where I had left off. "Oh Pumpkin," I said. "Your Lije is here." I had no real comfort to offer her, but at least I was there with her.

I didn't recall much of the rest of that day. A fog of despair, a black gloom, seemed to envelop my mind and soul. I only know that someone sewed the bodies of my parents and my brother into the sheets upon which they had slept. Someone trundled them into a wagon box and drove them to the growing cemetery. Someone preached a funeral sermon over the mounded earth. And then someone fed Mary Eliza and me a meal that night. Although the details were not clear, the charity of the Saints shone through my mind fog.

After a night spent huddled alongside my sister on a pallet on the stranger's floor, I arose with the dawn and went to clear our belongings from the cabin. Someone else's family would have need of it.

Chapter 15

Mary Eliza and I stayed with a succession of strangers in the next few days. Stunned as I was, however, I had to take action. I had decisions to make concerning Mary Eliza's and my life. I couldn't raise her alone. I couldn't mother her. I feared my grief would infect her. After days spent pleading with God for enlightenment, I came to the conclusion that I needed to find a temporary home for Mary Eliza while I rearranged our means of travel.

The two of us wouldn't require a wagon. I determined to sell the vehicle Pa and I had spent so much labor upon, along with our two yoke of oxen and our old horses, and seek out a friendly home for my sister while I went into Missouri to purchase a saddle horse for myself and Mary Eliza, and pack mules. It seemed like a good plan. A young man from the work party in which I had traveled to cut logs counseled me against entering that God-forsaken state, but as he had no authority over me beyond that of a casual friend, I paid him little heed.

I spoke to the mother of a little girl who had befriended Mary Eliza. I asked if she would consider taking my orphaned sister under her wing for a season while I carried out my plan. After she spoke to her husband, she agreed.

"Brother Marshall, I cannot bear to turn down your request. Brother Anson and I will do all in our power to comfort your little lass. She knows me. I think she will accept me."

The woman's kindly words and warm manner gave me assurance that I was on the right path. Within a week after I made my plan, I had sold my wagon and teams, said my tender farewell to Mary Eliza—who sobbed and clung to Sister Anson's skirt with a death grip—and turned my steps southward. I was obliged to dash tears from my eyes for a good hour after I made my departure.

~ ~ ~ ~ ~

I don't know how many days I traveled on foot into Missouri, for my mind was yet enwrapped with a cloud of grief. Never had I imagined that I would part company with my parents at such a young age. And to lose John besides! I had already endured the sorrow of Sarah's abandonment of her kin, but death? I could scarcely comprehend it.

One night I stayed at an inn outside a small town, taking a meal that hardly deserved the name. I slept on a pallet beside the fire, if the fitful hours of the night could be called rest. A party of three that had occupied a table in a corner throughout the evening, becoming drunk and rowdy, now snored with heads laid on crossed arms so close to a guttering lamp that I thought I smelled burning hair.

I arose, groggy and yawning, refused breakfast, paid my bill, and walked on down the road. Close upon noon, I entered a dense stand of trees, which blotted out the daylight to a great extent. Although my stomach grumbled, I determined to keep on my way until I reached the livestock dealer I had been told was nearby.

My mind was engaged in sorting out what to say to make the best deal on the animals I wanted to buy, when I was set upon from behind, my attackers raising a great commotion as they pummeled me with fists, clubs, and at least one sock filled with rocks. Not knowing but what my life and liberty were in danger, I fought with every trick I had used on John throughout our youth, but to no avail.

I must have fallen senseless to the road, for that is where I awoke what had to be hours later, my clothing torn and in disarray, my body bruised and sore, and my head bloodied. I spent some time getting my breath before I attempted to rise, and made use of the time searching for the pack I had carried upon my back.

I did not find it. I found instead the sock of rocks that had raised so many lumps upon my skull.

My head swam. Perhaps I had missed the pack because it was in the underbrush. I got to my feet and unsteadily made an investigation.

It wasn't there.

It wasn't under the trees on the other side of the road.

I slumped to the ground. I had been robbed.

~ ~ ~ ~ ~

"Come now, wake up."

Was I asleep? Why was I not dead? I shook my head, attempting to clear away the haze. The action brought pain, a headache like none I'd had before. Opening my eyes didn't relieve more than my doubt whether I lived or had passed beyond my mortal troubles. A man dressed in work-a-day clothing knelt over me in the twilight, smelling of hay and horses. How long had I lain senseless in the road?

I attempted to sit, and the man aided me in my pursuit. My hair obscured my vision, and I started to rake it back. Not only did my heedless fingers encounter numerous welts and bumps that protested vigorously against the intrusion, but my hair seemed stuck together with glue. I took in a noisy breath and removed my hand from my head.

"Bit of blood in your hair," the man observed. "We'll wash it out once I get you to my place."

After a while, he got me to my feet and walked me to his wagon. As I passed the team of horses, one stamped its feet and the other snorted. How much blood had I spilled upon my clothing to raise fear in them?

The wagon carried a high mound of hay, and the farmer half-hauled me up the wheel and onto the front-most part of the load. Then he clucked to the horses, and they put their shoulders into the harness and jerked the wagon into motion. I felt the lurch, not only in my head, but in many other portions of my person. Whoever had beaten me had done a thorough job of work. I refrained from moaning during the trip down the road, but not for want of doing so.

At last we arrived at a turnoff into a lane. We jostled over several places that had been washed out but not repaired. Having learned that biting my lip as a remedy against pain had bloody consequences, I gritted my teeth instead. Some of them moved a bit in their sockets, by which I surmised I had taken a good blow to the mouth.

"Ho," the man called to the horses. The wagon creaked and settled into rest. I smelled urine as the right-hand horse relieved itself.

"Mildred! Come help me."

A door at the side of the house opened and light spilled into the yard. "It's about time you're home, Marcus," a female voice called, moving closer as it spoke.

"Come around to the off side," the man said, and tugged me in that direction.

"What've you picked up this time?"

The man snorted. "Someone set upon this lad," he said, pulling me off the hay load and nearer to the edge of the wagon box. "He needs doctoring."

The woman muttered a surprised oath and reached up to receive my body.

I found myself clasped against a considerable bosom and held there by arms with strength to match. Then I felt myself being transferred into the arms of the farmer, who carried me through the door and into a large kitchen smelling of chicken and dumplings. Light flooded the room from a lamp hanging from the ceiling and another on a counter near a dishpan half-full of unwashed pots.

The woman took up the portable lamp and opened a door, which led into another room with a banked fireplace and several chairs. The farmer set me down in one of them, an armchair covered in fabric woven from horsehair. He didn't seem to mind that my clothing was covered with dust and clotted blood. I vaguely wondered if the missus was of a like mind, or if my condition was an affront to her sensibilities.

She only said, "Get them horses out of harness. I'll tend to the boy."

~ ~ ~ ~ ~

I spent a week under Mildred Earnshaw's care, lying on a pallet near the hearth, worrying over my situation. Had I brought the attack upon myself by not taking better heed of my father's injunction to follow the leaders to Zion? I still didn't know where Zion was located, but perhaps my plan for this detour was ill-considered. It had felt right at the time I made it, but maybe I had been misled by my feelings of desperation and grief.

I missed my sister. I missed my parents. I missed John.

Occasionally, a thin boy about fifteen years of age—who was introduced to me as the Earnshaw's son, Harold—helped me partake of my meals: broth at first, then gruel, then more substantial food. By the end of the week, I no longer experienced dizziness, palpitations, or a sick stomach when I sat up. I figured I knew how my father had felt as he recovered. I no longer wished to lie about, feeling indolent and useless.

I arose before dawn on the eighth day, and finding my clothing, washed and mended and folded in a stack near to my bedside, dressed myself and went outdoors to find the outhouse.

Having taken care of my functions, I noticed a cord or so

of wood stacked against the wall of the house, with an axe sunk into a cut-off stump of a log meant for chopping. I removed the axe, replaced it with a length of wood, and set about making fuel.

Although my muscles had weakened from lack of use, the satisfaction of using them until they were warm and supple gave me a curious joy.

I hadn't felt joy for a long while, and welcomed it as a temporary replacement for my anxiety over losing my money and belongings. Eventually, I would have to sort out what I was to do to obtain the animals that I had come to Missouri to buy. In the meantime, I savored the emotion while it occupied my heart and mind.

When I had cut a good armload of wood, I sent the axe deep into the stump, picked up the wood, and entered the house.

"There you are," said Mr. Earnshaw. "I knew you had the look of a worker."

"I'm no stranger to labor," I said as I deposited half the load in the wood box beside the hearth. I proceeded into the kitchen, and topped off the box beside the stove.

Mrs. Earnshaw stirred eggs in a skillet, following my movements with her gaze. "So you're mended," she said.

"Yes, ma'am. What else can I do for you?"

She motioned with her spoon. "You can sit yourself at the table and eat."

"Yes, ma'am," I repeated, and hastened to obey. The woman was unlike my mother in every way but one. She had a kind heart underneath her bluff and sizeable exterior.

As we ate, Mr. Earnshaw questioned me about my history and purpose for traveling in those parts.

I shifted in my seat. With no desire for animosity from these folks, I decided to leave out a few details. "I came down from Iowa to buy a horse and mules so I can go west," I said.

"West, huh? Do you have family in Iowa? I suppose

you're striking out on your own." He put a forkful of food in his mouth and chewed.

"Only a sister," I muttered. "My folks are recently dead." I filled my mouth with food so I wouldn't have to expand my explanation.

"That's a cause for grief," Mrs. Earnshaw said. "I give you my condolences."

I nodded in agreement. "Thank you, ma'am." My gut felt hollow.

"Where's the girl?" Mr. Earnshaw asked.

"A family took her in." I suppressed a grimace of pain at the thought of my little sister all alone with the Anson family.

Mr. Earnshaw stroked his chin. "You didn't have any belongings when I picked you up. Did your attackers take them?"

"Yes, sir. It appears they stole my pack."

"And your money with it?"

I felt my throat close. "Yes, sir," I finally managed to get out.

"Now you sit at my table with no means to purchase animals." He drummed his fingers on the tabletop. "Does it matter when you go west?"

I considered his question. I couldn't leave this season. It was too late in the year to make the journey. I didn't know where he was heading with his question, but I might as well answer honestly. "No, sir, I don't suppose it does."

"Well then." He leaned back in his chair. "You don't fear hard work. If you will stay and do chores with me for a year, I will give you a good horse and mule and you can be on your way west."

It seemed like a fair bargain, but an entire year away from my sister? If I were going to get us equipped for the trek, it had to be so. I rose and shook Mr. Earnshaw's hand. "Thank you, sir."

"I won't mention to the neighbors that you're a

Mormon," he said, still gripping my hand.

"What?" I hadn't said a word on that topic, as far as I knew. Had something slipped out when I was unconscious?

Mr. Earnshaw released my hand. "I found a few pages from the beginning of your holy book scattered on the ground, but I have no quarrel with the Mormons. I settled here after they left. This place was abandoned, and I got it for back taxes."

~ ~ ~ ~ ~

After I had passed a few weeks in Mr. Earnshaw's employ, I thought to write a letter to the Anson family explaining the reason for my delay in returning. However, when I asked how mail was handled in the vicinity, my benefactor discovered my desire and strongly advised me against sending mail to Mount Pisgah.

"That is known as a Mormon town, Elijah. You don't want to alert the folks around here to your true religious affiliation. We've gone to pains to avoid the subject."

I suffered pains, as well, that I could not safely let Sister Anson know I had not abandoned Mary Eliza, but would return in a year. I had no contact with my sister or any other person in Iowa during my entire stay in Missouri.

As to my religious worship, I attended church services with the Earnshaw family, feeling a deep sense of disgust with myself for being a pretender. I hoped God was mindful of the reason for my subterfuge. Even so, I did not partake of the sacramental emblems used in their services. I dared not do it. According to my understanding, my action would be a grave insult to Him.

Although harvest was not yet upon us, the time finally arrived when my year of labor for Mr. Earnshaw had come to an end. Harold had gained sufficient stature and strength that I knew I would not be leaving his father without help.

I myself had put on one or two stone of weight, my chest had broadened, and my muscles had hardened beyond their adolescent state. With several additional inches in height, as well, I could truly say that I had achieved the stature of a man.

How I yearned to see Mary Eliza again!

Accordingly, at the supper table one night I broached the subject of obtaining my reward and taking my leave.

Mr. Earnshaw paused with his fork halfway to his mouth. After a moment, he set down the utensil and took a deep breath. "I've grown fond of you," he said. "I'd come to think of you as my own son, and hoped you would forget your desire to leave us. Every time I drive down the lane, I'm thankful I came upon you and brought you home."

He referred to the job I had done repairing the roadbed, using a pickaxe on the stubborn earth so I could smooth it down to a level surface.

Mrs. Earnshaw got up from the table, saying she'd forgotten to serve something, but I knew it was a ploy to hide her feelings. Contrary to apprehensions I'd suffered at the beginning of our relationship, I had gotten along quite amicably with the Earnshaw family, and felt pangs of regret at the thought of leaving. As I had no parents, and little family beyond my younger sister, I'd become comfortable thinking of them as suitable substitutes.

I flicked a glance at Harold. He was as different from John as night from day, but for the past year, we had shared a bond of brotherhood that would be difficult to replace. I tried to ignore his hangdog expression. Instead, I focused on the fact that I had received a charge from my mother to see after Mary Eliza. Although I had taken a necessary detour, it was time I got back on the track to Zion.

"I must leave," I said. "Mary Eliza is waiting for me."

Mr. Earnshaw nodded and sighed, but agreed that as payment for my year of labor, on the morrow I should have possession of a fine horse and mule, and provisions to see me back to Iowa.

Chapter 16

After a journey of some days, I arrived back in Mount Pisgah. The place had grown. Fields of buckwheat glistened golden in the hot sun, tidy fences marching around them, more rows of cabins on each end of the fields, wells with sturdy heads interspersed among the homes, and roads packed down between the houses.

I had to pause to get my bearings, but once I had decided where it was, I hastened to the cabin where the Anson family dwelled.

After I knocked on the door, my emotions almost overcame me right there on the stoop. I was to be reunited with Mary Eliza at last. I heard footsteps from within and tried to calm the rapid beating of my heart.

A woman opened the door. My greeting of "Mother Anson" died on my lips. A stranger stood before me, wiping her hands on her apron with the undeniable air of the mistress of the house. I felt my grin wither.

"Hello," the woman said. "What can I do for you?" Her accent felt strange entering my ears.

I took several breaths before I could stammer my answer. "I'm looking—I need—uh, where is Mother Anson?"

The woman raised an eyebrow at me. "Why, the Anson's left in springtime, before we came along. I must say they left the house in right good order."

British, I thought. Then reality intruded. *Mary Eliza's*

gone! "That can't be," I exclaimed. "They had my sister in their care." Cold fear ran through my spine.

"Well, I wouldn't know about that, now would I. You'd best go ask after your sister in Winter Quarters, ain't that so?"

"I thank you," I said through numb lips, and stumbled off the stoop.

I spent the night in a cold, damp, empty cabin, wrapped in a blanket Mildred Earnshaw had given me. I had been unable to get my stiff fingers to strike a fire.

When morning came, I headed westward to find Mary Eliza. I had learned only one thing about Winter Quarters: it was the settlement on the far side of the Missouri River where the Saints who arrived too late to go west spent the season of dark and cold. If my sister and the Anson family had been delayed in their travels from Mount Pisgah to there, I might be able to catch up to them. That was my fervent hope.

~ ~ ~ ~ ~

Two long weeks later, I arrived at dusk on the eastern bank of the Missouri River. My horse had pulled up lame in the wilds of Iowa, and I was obliged to rest him before continuing on my way, slowly, to accommodate the horse's impairment.

I camped that night near the ferry, wishing I could swim my horse and mule over the river and begin my search for Mary Eliza. That would be folly in the twilight, and besides, I'd been told the Missouri was a capricious river.

When morning came, I stood in line to get on the ferry, my money jingling ready in my hand to pay for the crossing. At last, a wagon with its occupants was light enough that I could join them with my animals, and my heart began to race at the prospect of greeting my sister again. How tall would she be now? Would she remember me? Would she forgive me for leaving her with the Ansons?

Anxiety stole through my soul as I waited out the water crossing to be able to disembark on the far shore. What if the Ansons had left Mary Eliza behind with another family in Mount Pisgah? Why hadn't I checked before I left there? I could not imagine Mother Anson doing such a thing, but I was not well acquainted with her spouse, and had no knowledge of how he made decisions for his family. Perhaps he saw my sister as a burden. I told myself that wasn't possible. Sister Anson had not agreed to my proposal until she had discussed it with her husband. With a sense of relief, I had assumed her positive acceptance of my plan had meant the husband was agreeable, too. On the other hand, I had been delayed in returning to Mount Pisgah, and had been too much of a coward to write a letter, esteeming my life and liberty as more important than Mary Eliza's. What had I done?

These painful thoughts ran through my mind until the ferry bumped against the log landing. The impact pulled me from my self-castigation long enough for me to tend to my animals' departure from the boat.

Now what was I to do?

Attempting to leave my quandary on the river bank, I set off toward the most populous area of Winter Quarters. I hoped to find there a person in charge, an office with records, some place where I could obtain knowledge of the whereabouts of Mary Eliza.

I spent two days combing the streets of the settlement, for it held several hundreds of cabins and I was weary. I finally found a small office tucked away in the back room of a dry goods establishment. The gentleman ensconced behind a desk greeted me with a measure of reservation, but after much exertion on my part to persuade him to share his knowledge, determined that yes, a family named Anson had arrived in the spring and dwelt for a month in the town before leaving in a company headed for Zion.

"Do you have an enumeration of the family members?" I asked, anxiety buffeting me.

"Well, yes. Brother and Sister Anson, accompanied by two girls and three boys."

I knew of only one girl in the family. "But names, do you have their names?"

The brother shook his head. "Only how many members comprised the family is in the notation."

My heart seemed to contract, and pain flooded my bosom.

He must have seen how poorly I took the news, for he said, "Perhaps you can question the people where the Ansons lived. I understand only one of two families in the house left this spring."

Hope loosened my heart. "Where do I find them?"

He gave me the particulars of how I was to locate the Philips family, and I departed, rather more hastily than was polite.

I found the residence with little trouble, and when Sister Philips answered the door, I made an inquiry about the past inhabitants, in particular, the girl called Mary Eliza.

"She was a quiet little thing," the woman informed me. "Very shy. So different from her sister."

"And you're sure that was her name?"

The sister looked startled. "Why yes. Why wouldn't it be?"

"She is *my* sister," I answered. "No kin of the Ansons." A cold breeze whipped down the street and under my coattail. Realization dawned that I could not expect to leave for the west this season in order to find her. "I thank you for your information," I said, disappointment coating my tongue like sulfur.

~ ~ ~ ~ ~

With no hope of going west until the following spring, I could only wait out the fall and winter, and join a company when the grass came again. I went about the settlement, trying to get lodgings, but was told the Saints were pulling out of Winter Quarters soon, it being on Indian land. I should return across the river if I desired to find a place to stay for the winter.

Accordingly, I got back on the ferry and eventually found housing with a family named Grant in the new settlement of Kanesville. Brother Grant owned a wagon shop and needed a workman. I could build wagons, so I applied for the job and won it, beating out three other applicants as qualified as I. Very much grateful, I endeavored to make myself useful to the man and to his missus at their home, as well.

The first time I attended Sabbath services, I almost wept at the opportunity to partake of the body and blood of Christ once more. I restrained my emotion with difficulty, and sat back afterward to enjoy the sermonizing. A choir concluded the meeting with a hymn, which put me in mind of John and how much joy he had received from song.

As I worked at my job, I had much time for pondering on my life and the mishaps therein: Sarah's flight, the deaths of my family members, the enforced absence from my younger sister. By turns I was joyful or grief stricken, depending on whether my mind wandered onto a gospel topic full of hope, or if I wondered how God would view my mistakes and trespasses. I surely bore blame for teasing and tormenting my older sister, and suffered some great turmoil over the matter. I sorely needed a diversion from such thoughts.

I found it when Brigham Young and part of the pioneer company returned to Iowa as October slid into November. I learned that Brother Brigham had recognized the Great Salt Lake Valley as God's chosen location for Zion.

The Great Salt Lake Valley? Where was that?

Brother Brigham often spoke at church services in and around Kanesville, and I tried to avail myself of the opportunity to attend any meeting in which he would participate. Besides hoping to discover more about our new Zion, I needed the spirit I felt when in his presence, as it comforted me in my afflictions and eased my sense of guilt for all my failings.

From the meetings I attended, I learned that the Great Salt Lake Valley contained a vast lake of salt and lay within the confines of the Great Basin. The valley was situated west of the Wasatch Range of the Rocky Mountains, but east of California. It was a secluded place, a plain dotted with sagebrush bushes and other desert vegetation. No other people had claimed it, save for roaming bands of Indians.

It sounded somewhat austere, but the pioneer company had broken ground for crops. About two thousand Saints had departed from Winter Quarters since the spring. I hoped that when I managed to get to Zion, there was still land to be had. All I wanted was to find Mary Eliza, obtain land and begin to farm.

~ ~ ~ ~ ~

I had by now become well settled into the age of nineteen, and felt an increasing interest in the fairer sex. Someday I wished to find a good woman to court and marry, and to raise a family. Although Brother Brigham and other church leaders had several wives, I would need only one.

Over the years since I left the valley in Pennsylvania, I learned that the tale of twenty-five wives that Hans Stiles had whispered to Sarah was a gross exaggeration of the facts.

God had indeed commanded some of the brethren of the church, like Brother Brigham, to marry more than one wife. This uncomfortable duty became necessary to care for the many single ladies who joined with the Saints in larger numbers than had single men.

Perhaps the second reason—to raise a righteous generation to the Lord—bore even more importance. The church must grow in strength and numbers to prevent such persecutions as had come upon it in the past. That had to be why the Saints were settling in the valley of the Great Salt Lake. Although it might seem somewhat desolate, it was quite promising as an out-of-the-way place to raise crops and build homes and industry. To my understanding, there was room in the Great Basin to accommodate the future growth of the Saints.

I hoped that through the expenditure of much labor, one day I would have a home to offer to a woman. While I had no desire for more than one wife, I no longer thought to censure those who were called to enter into more than a single marriage covenant.

I found diversion of another sort that winter when the Grant family put on a dance party in their home to celebrate a thanksgiving time. One of the young ladies present seemed to be attracted to me. I felt unworthy of her esteem, but I needed to overcome a decided shyness on my part when in company with a lady.

This particular young lady, who was called Matilda Wainswright, accepted my invitation to dance a number of times throughout the evening. Although her eyes sparkled and her features were comely, I did not feel drawn to her in any great measure. Still, as I danced with her, I was able to gain needed confidence.

~ ~ ~ ~ ~

In Kanesville, the Saints were building a commodious tabernacle made of logs. It was rumored that the hurry with which this enterprise was being conducted was so that a general conference could be held very soon. It was further rumored that a great announcement would be forthcoming at the conference. With the community abuzz, I could not dwell on my sorrows. The excitement infected me, and I eagerly awaited whatever grand plan would be given.

When the day arrived for the first session of the conference, I could not attend for the press of work in the wagon shop. Gulping down my disappointment, I toiled throughout the day building wagon boxes.

Finally, two days after Christmas, our workload eased, and I was able to crowd into the tabernacle, so new it still smelled of pine.

When Brother Brigham took the stand, my heart swelled until I choked. As President of the Quorum of Twelve Apostles, he had led the church for the past three years, and had done a noble job. I held my breath, waiting for whatever he would propose in this conference.

He started out simply, telling us that the Church needed a full complement of leaders. We would be much better served from now on with a First Presidency, Quorum of the Twelve, and a Patriarch to the Church. By now, I breathed regularly, but remembered wondering who would be the new Patriarch when, three years past, William Smith had been ejected from the position. Evidently, the time had come for it to be filled.

My greater excitement, however, was reserved for what Brother Brigham had said about a new First Presidency. The church hadn't had one since my family arrived in Nauvoo to discover that our prophet and his brother had been killed in a dastardly fashion.

When Brother Brigham had said his piece, another man, Orson Pratt by name, arose and presented Brigham Young as the new President of the Church. We were asked for our approval, which caused a hubbub as we all raised our right hands and murmured to our neighbors. Next, President Young presented the names of Heber C. Kimball and Willard Richards as his counselors, and the consenting vote was unanimous, as before. After many other names were given for other quorums and we had sustained them in their positions, John Smith's name was read as the new Patriarch to the Church.

Strong emotion surged through me at hearing the beloved leader's name, and I did not hold it back. "Uncle"

John had been the stake president in Nauvoo. Now he held the birthright office of Patriarch, and a spirit whispered to me that all was well.

I choked on a sob at recognizing my father's familiar phrase of comfort. How I longed to hear once more his dear voice repeat those words. I knew it could not be, but I was comforted, nonetheless.

When I left the tabernacle, I walked with a light step back to the Grant's home, rejoicing that the Church had been set to rights again. Despite my absence from my sister, for the moment, all was well.

Chapter 17

Spring came. The ice broke up on the river, flowing downstream in mighty chunks that threatened shipping and ferries alike. On the prairies surrounding the settlements, grass sprang up and trees budded in greeting of the new season.

By now I had a small sack hidden beneath my mattress in which I had put by wages enough to purchase supplies for my journey west. I could hardly wait to go, was more than willing to set out across the plains toward the setting sun. My only difficulty lay in securing a spot in one of the companies that would leave this spring or summer.

The members of the new First Presidency each had charge of a company of wagons. I applied for a place in that of President Young, but more than one thousand souls had gotten ahead of me and would depart under his command towards the end of May. Then I tried for a spot with President Kimball's cohort, but it too was filled to capacity.

Finally, as my last hope waned, I secured a position as an ox team driver in the division headed by President Richards, he who had witnessed the deaths of Hyrum and Joseph Smith. My ruffled feelings at not being able to journey in association with the new prophet were considerably soothed when I learned that our company would bring along a cannon.

Prior to our departure, which was to take place on June thirtieth, we were to make our way to the Elkhorn River, a number of miles west of the Missouri, from which we would launch ourselves into the void.

I purchased supplies enough to get me across the Great Plains and sustain me for a length of time in my new location in Zion. The mound of goods would overwhelm my lone mule, so I scouted around for a second, and was fortunate to find one for sale from a brother who had decided oxen would serve him better than mules to draw his wagon. Loaded up at last, I set out for the gathering place on the Elkhorn and arrived without mishap on the day before we were to depart.

I found the wagon for which I was employed as driver and met the family that owned it, surnamed Rasmussen. The head of the family had a malformed leg and could not drive his own yokes of oxen, but his unhappy circumstance afforded me the opportunity to travel over the Zion trail this season.

I next attended a reading of the rules of the camp from the mouth of Brother John Armstrong, who was captain over the ten families with which I would travel. Some of the important rules were that we should observe good order in the camp, not shout to one another, meet together nightly for prayers, and extinguish all lights by nine p.m. Conditions permitting, we would not travel on the Sabbath. A further instruction of note was directed toward those of us who were employed as oxen drivers: we must stay at the side of our yoked teams at all times, until we were permitted to leave them.

That evening, our company of ten assembled for prayers. Although I was a single man, I was lumped into the lot because of my job as a driver for one of the families. I looked over the gathering. I was the only man of my status, which caused me a bit of discomfort, for I knew none of these people. I could only hope they were decent sorts and would make me welcome.

After Captain Armstrong beseeched the Heavenly Father for a safe journey on the morrow, I expected that when the final "amen" had been said, we would disperse to our individual beds and take what sleep our anxieties would permit us. However, as we rose from our knees, one brother began singing a song unfamiliar to me. I listened as he lifted his voice in exhortation to cast out fear, and instead let joy accompany us on our way. As he ended, his final words rang in my ears: "All is well. All is well."

As I got into my bedroll, I thought of my father. His faith ever led him to encourage me and my siblings, as well as my mother, with that phrase. Despite his hopes and dreams, he would never see Zion. I must get there in his place, find my sister, and care for her as though she were my own child.

~ ~ ~ ~ ~

We started out well enough, with our company of ten traveling in the first division of the larger company of about one hundred wagons. There being two divisions, we had around fifty wagons that traveled in close company, but further divided into our smaller groups of ten. Captain Armstrong had charge over the 3rd Ten, as it was called, so we were placed near the middle of the division.

The second division started behind us. We kept them in sight all day until the waning of the afternoon, when they fell behind us. Perhaps they were forced to stop for an emergency.

Throughout the day, I worried over the abundance of small children walking beside the wagons. Being children, they took occasion to chase each other from time to time, darting between the wagons, often so close to the oncoming yokes of oxen as to take my breath from me. I prayed that no harm would come to the little ones from my team.

We made fifteen miles of travel the first day, and camped after crossing a slough, where we had to double our teams to get through the encumbering weeds and water. I thought I had done a fine job of driving the oxen, for we kept up with the others. I also had avoided running down any small people.

I unyoked the oxen, hobbled them on a good grazing ground, then returned to camp to make my supper.

Brother Rasmussen said, "You eat with us, ya?"

I didn't know my position included board, but scarcely was of a mind to turn the brother down. Although I knew my way around kitchen implements, I welcomed a meal made by another person.

Sister Rasmussen was an amply-built woman, which I found was a testament to her good cooking. After the meal, we had evening prayer by companies of ten, and went to bed, dousing the lights a few minutes after the hour of nine o'clock. It being our first night on the trail, I hoped no one would be cantankerous about our lack of punctuality.

I spent a restless night, being awakened time and again by a child in our ten who coughed and wheezed until I could hardly stand the distressed noise. I hoped the child had croup, for if it was afflicted with whooping cough, we might have a serious outbreak of poor health.

A horn awakened our division at four a.m. I gathered my bedroll and stowed it, then went out to bring in the oxen. In my haste, I missed morning prayers, for which I was reprimanded. I vowed never to bring Captain Armstrong's ire down upon me again, at least not for that misdeed.

The second day of travel passed without incident. Having traversed sixteen miles, we made camp, took care of our duties, and sought our beds to refresh ourselves for the morrow.

I was not granted a night of rest. Two children passed the night trumpeting their throats raw. I wondered if, on future nights, I should have to take myself out into the wilds in order to sleep.

Again the horn blew at four a.m., and I repeated my camp-breaking efforts as before, except that I did attend the proscribed prayers.

We traveled only six miles that day, as we were obliged to cross a rocky stream, then endured a severe storm of wind and rain, into which the captain of our division felt we'd best not try to venture.

Accordingly, we camped beside the stream, which rose in the night, flooding the ground where we had staked the cattle to graze. After we moved the oxen to another area, I spent a miserable night in wet clothes and blankets, listening to harsh sounds from three or more children.

I awoke to find the Rasmussen family very poor of health and spirits, for one of their children had died in the night, and another was close upon doing so. Moreover, I discovered that the amplified sounds of the night before had come, not from another child as I had supposed, but from the father of the family, who still lay in his blankets.

This alarmed not only Sister Rasmussen, but me, as well. We held council with Captain Armstrong, whose opinion of sickness in the camp was disapproving, to say the least. I wondered if the man had ever seen a sick day himself, for he seemed lacking in understanding for the plight of the Rasmussens.

"If your man dies, you'll have to turn back," he told the grieving mother. "But we'd better bury your son here, before others fall ill."

So it was done. I took a good portion of the labor of digging a grave for the child upon myself. It was finished and a brief ceremony completed before we left for the day's journey.

I walked beside the ox team for fifteen long miles that day, listening to whooping sounds coming from the wagon. In the afternoon, one voice became faint, and the other stopped. I knew I would dig at least one more grave that evening.

By the time I unyoked the oxen, my dire task had become preparing a burial site for two.

~ ~ ~ ~ ~

Instead of the customary horn, the sound of a cannon firing off awoke us the following morning. I flexed my sore arms and wondered at the occasion. Only later in the day did I recall the date, July Fourth.

Sister Rasmussen didn't know much English, but she knew the word "no." She refused to let me return with her to Kanesville, repeating, "I drive, I drive." After I lost the argument, she turned her face to the east, whipped up her oxen, and left her babies and her husband behind in the prairie soil. I imagined she preferred to be alone with her grief.

Captain Armstrong as much as shrugged his shoulders and let her go, unaccompanied. I wished we had a less unfeeling man at our head, but at least he did not insist that I go back to Iowa to stay until another season had passed. I assured him I had supplies, and he agreed that I could travel on.

That day I rode my horse for the first time since we had set off, and at the beginning, I had a frisky time of it. The animal must have decided it enjoyed its unburdened state, and thus couldn't be bothered to transport me without putting up a protest. I was not an accomplished horseman, but I came out conqueror at last, and caught up to my company before they had traveled more than a few miles ahead of me.

When we camped, I noticed more sickness had overtaken members of our group. I spent the next three days driving the oxen of a Brother Wilson. Fortunately for him, he recovered his health and I was back to taming my mount in the mornings. I felt fortunate myself that I no longer had to listen to Sister Wilson's shrewish tongue castigating her poor spouse for taking sick. If spells of feeling like a stranger in this company came upon me in the future, I would remember to give thanks that I was not intimate friends with the Wilson family.

We journeyed on, crossing streams and meeting people coming from the other direction. Among them were men from the Mormon Battalion, returning to Iowa to assemble their families for a trek to Zion. One night, two men carrying mail back to the Saints camped with us. I always took such occasions to speak with men who came from the Salt Lake Valley to discover if they knew the Anson family. Thus far, no one could give me news of them.

The next day about noon, a brother in our Ten collapsed beside his oxen. I heard a voice scream, "Joshua," then a slim woman clambered down from the moving wagon at great risk to herself and ran to his side. By the time I could get there, she knelt in the dust, cradling his head in her arms, rocking back and forth as a small voice from the wagon cried, "Mama, Mama."

I got the animals halted, and then went to see if I could be of assistance. When I arrived at the side of the couple, it was clear to me from the color of the man's skin that he was beyond mortal help.

Needless to say, our group halted early for the day. I hadn't thought to put my new-found grave digging skills to use again so soon. Another brother took his turn with me, and between us, we put Joshua Porter in his grave.

Chapter 18

Sister Porter trembled slightly as she stood before Captain Armstrong, who glared up at her from underneath his bushy eyebrows.

It made my heart ache to see her standing there by the flickering campfire, leaning forward in her anxiety to learn why the captain had called her to his fire. She cast a slim shadow from the uncertain light, but that was as it should be. She couldn't be over eighteen, and had only borne one child that I knew anything about. Her husband, his journey done, lay out under the prairie sod, leaving her a widow with a son only just beginning to walk.

The captain sat on a keg of flour where he had been whittling on a stick before the widow arrived to learn her fate. After a long moment, he tossed the stick into the fire and shifted himself on the keg.

"Sister Porter, you may think it a harsh thing, but I have to consider the welfare of all the families in my care. Now that Brother Porter is gone, you can't possibly keep up. You've got to return to Iowa."

He looked around the circle at all of us who had scurried over to observe the spectacle. When he saw me, he stopped his survey and gazed at me for a while. Then he nodded, as though to himself, and continued. "It's only about two weeks' travel back to Kanesville. I'll send Brother Marshall here along to see you get there safe." He stopped and looked into the fire, then shrugged. "You can go to Zion next season, after you get someone to take charge of your wagon."

My surprise at having my future so suddenly changed by a few offhand words was soon overtaken by my ire. What did Captain Armstrong intend that I should do? Twiddle my thumbs in Iowa for another year? No. I had already been put to great pains to get to Zion this season. Mary Eliza was waiting, and I did not care to have our reunion delayed. I meant to continue westward, in this company or without it. I glared at the captain, but he did not look at me again.

Instead, he fumbled with his clasp knife, finally got it closed, then stuffed it into his vest pocket. Sister Porter twisted her hands in the cloth of her apron. The captain looked at her bleak face, and then cleared his throat.

"A lone woman can't manage this trek by herself," he said.

I knew different. A widow with three half-grown children, who traveled in the second division, was making the journey by herself.

It didn't make a particle of sense for Captain Armstrong to send this despairing woman back to Iowa in my care when we could press forward instead, and both arrive in the Valley of the Great Salt Lake this season.

I swallowed down my anger, took off my old black hat, and stepped out of the shadows into the firelight. "Captain, I believe Sister Porter would prefer to travel onward. I can just as well see her to Zion as to Iowa."

All the eyes of the assembled Saints moved in my direction, and I stared back at them, challenging them to dispute my words.

The young widow took a step forward, and I looked her way. She looked back at me, surprise evident on her face. I had not consulted with her on the matter.

As I watched, she straightened her posture. My offer

evidently gave her hope. She gave me a slight nod, accepting my proposal.

I raked my hair back from my forehead and gave her a nod in return. I put my hat back on my head and turned to see if our accord was acceptable to the Captain.

Relief spread over John Armstrong's wide face. He said to me, "If it won't put you out of your way, I'm sure Sister Porter is grateful for your help." He waved a dismissive hand, got up from his keg, and disappeared into the darkness.

I blew out a breath of air. I would get to the promised valley this year.

~ ~ ~ ~ ~

The Saints melted away into the shadows surrounding the campfire. I turned to the widow. She stared at me, curiosity in her look, but a wariness of me too, for she had just that day seen me put her husband into the ground. My offer had to make her uncomfortable, for all its value to her.

I doffed my hat again and nodded to her, shyness overcoming my tongue of a sudden and whisking away the words I had planned to speak.

A moment passed, silence holding a barrier between us.

She lifted her hand, palm toward me. "I thank you for your kindness," she managed to say, and closed her fingers. "I know that Captain Armstrong meant well, but I can't wait another year to go to Zion." Her voice broke then, and she finished in a whisper. "I have no place else to go."

By now her lifted hand had descended to wring the other. Her face twisted a bit, and I feared she would cry, but she mastered the emotion and calmed her countenance again.

I found my tongue. "Is there anything you need me to do tonight?"

"No. Now that my future's settled, I can get on with supper." She hesitated for a moment, then looked me in the eye. "Won't you come to the fire and eat with us when supper's ready?"

Her offer surprised me, but I wasn't about to refuse a meal cooked by a hand other than my own. "I'd like that. You can give me instructions for the morrow." I nodded to her, put back on my hat, and said, "I'll see you at your fire by and by."

She moved away from the fire toward her own wagon. I turned and went to where I had staked out my animals, intent upon moving them to a new patch of grass. The work gave me a chance to reflect on what I had talked myself into doing. Here I was, a lone man of only twenty years of age, on my way to Zion to find my sister. Now, because I thought a man had treated a woman unfairly, I also had taken upon myself the care of that woman and her child, with the responsibility of getting her safe to the valley.

When I finished with my horse and mules, I went to the widow's fire and accepted a plate from her hand. The boy, who was seated on a blanket spread upon the earth, began to fuss. She went to him, set her half-eaten meal aside, and picked him up.

By her furtive actions, I discovered that she needed to nurse her child, but my presence had put her in somewhat of a quandary. I turned away, a bit embarrassed, to allow her the privacy she needed to put the matter to rights. Of course I had seen my mother nurse Mary Eliza, but that had been years previous, and this woman wasn't family. After sufficient time had elapsed that I figured she had remedied the situation, I glanced around. To my relief, the problem was resolved. I found a seat on the ground and tucked into my meal.

From time to time as I ate, I glanced up at Sister Porter. I could not be sure, due to the dancing of the small light cast by her fire, but it seemed to me that her eyes were somewhat swollen and reddened. I caught her brushing a tear from her cheek. She turned her head away and snuggled her nursing son, obviously aware of my gaze.

I admired the woman. That under such circumstances as these she had prepared a meal for herself and for a stranger, too, was a thing of no small moment to me. She had a determination to endure to the end, no matter what the cost. At the same time, I felt powerless. There was no way a stranger such as I could ease her sorrow. I ducked my head to my meal once again, wishing for a way to relieve her pain.

By the time I had eaten the last morsel from the tin plate, I knew of one task I could take over tonight. I stood and carried my plate, the utensils, and my cup over to the washtub sitting atop a barrel. I removed my hat and rolled up my sleeves before she realized that I intended to wash the dishes.

As I plunged my hands into the water, I heard the rustle of fabric as she regulated her attire. She must have put the boy on his blanket and got to her feet, for the next thing I knew, she stood at my side at the washtub.

"Brother Marshall." Her voice held a note of distress. "That's my chore. I will clean up later."

I looked down at her and smiled in a way I hoped was reassuring. "I have long practice of the task, Sister. Let me take this way of paying you back for the meal. It was far better fare than I usually stir up." I smiled again, hoping she would not press further to do the job herself.

She returned to her seat and picked up her plate. I circled the tub until I could see her as I went about the work. She remained silent. I was curious to know if I had cheered her, at least to a small degree.

She finally lifted her head and looked my way. Her gaze was direct. It disturbed me in an odd way.

"Why did you speak up to help me go to Zion? You scarcely know me."

~ ~ ~ ~ ~

I hadn't expected her question. I scrubbed at a cup and dipped it into the rinse water before I answered. "He was unkind. He didn't want to deal with you." I shook the water from the cup and wiped it with a flour sack. "You were suddenly alone, and I remember how that felt." I rubbed my hands dry on the sack and returned to my seat on the ground. I should have left, but I sensed that she needed company.

"Your wife died?" She whispered the question.

My ears burned, and I leaned back, my shoulders tight, before replying. "I never had a wife. It was my folks and my brother I lost, back in Mount Pisgah. They got taken by the cholera."

"I'm sorry." She stirred the remains of her food.

I noticed that a lock of hair had escaped the roll at the nape of her neck, hung beside her cheek, and moved with her motion. It was light brown, but the firelight caught glints of red in the tendril.

"I don't even know your name, beyond 'Brother Marshall'," she added.

"Elijah. Most folks just call me 'Lije'." I felt my muscles loosen.

She gestured toward her boy. "This is Joseph." She inhaled sharply, then went on. "When they don't call me 'Sister Porter,' folks call me 'Etta'. That's short for 'Henrietta'." She noticed the loose hair and attempted to put it back into its place.

I picked up my hat and dangled it from two fingers. I wanted to go, but she still hungered for conversation, so I stayed. I shifted one foot. "That's a fine name."

"I've never heard of anybody named Elijah, except the Bible prophet. Did your folks give you his name?"

I laughed. "No. My pa and ma were God-fearing folk, but that wasn't the case. They named me for my grandpa."

She smiled. The action transformed her face. I'd brought pleasure to her. The child sighed, and she glanced down.

"I expect I'd best get along," I said. "You'll be needing to tuck that youngster into bed." I stood up.

She aimed that direct gaze up at me. "Wait . . . Lije."

A shiver went through me to hear a woman of her station call my name. I wasn't prepared for that, even though we'd exchanged Christian names.

She continued. "We didn't talk about what needs doing tomorrow."

"That's right, ma'am."

Her forehead furrowed. "I'm not so old as that. Please sit down."

I sat. I resolved not to refer to her as "ma'am" again.

"I won't need you to drive the team. Joshua—Brother Porter—taught me how in case . . . in case anything happened to him." She stopped for a moment, and I saw the pain in her eyes.

After a time I said, "I dislike seeing you walk when you could ride in the wagon with the child. Captain Armstrong will think I went back on my word."

"If he says anything, I will make sure he knows different. I won't be a burden to anyone. Only . . . keep your eye out for trouble. Please." Then her voice lowered in pitch. "Could you lend a hand crossing the rivers? I—" She looked down for a moment. "I have a fear of water."

"I'll watch out for you. I've put my word to it." I got to my feet. "Goodnight, Sister Porter."

~ ~ ~ ~ ~

I was invited to the widow's supper fire every night for a week. I enjoyed our conversations and playing with her little son, coaxing him to toddle between us. Once he looked at his mother and said, "Mama." Then he pointed to me and called out, "Papa!"

I know my face colored as I took him into my arms and replied, "No, I'm Lije."

That night after the communal prayer of our Ten, Sister Porter asked me to walk her back to her wagon and join in her evening prayer. I hesitated, but saw that she felt low.

Perhaps saying a prayer with her would comfort her tonight.

We knelt beside the wagon with Joseph asleep in his blanket between us. Sister Porter began to pray aloud, telling the Father that she sorrowed and asking that he send the Holy Ghost as a comfort to her. She fell silent for a while, and I wondered if she expected me to take up the prayer. Just as I opened my mouth, she continued.

"I thank thee for the company of Brother Elijah. He brings calm with him."

My eyebrows rose as I opened my eyes to stare at her. Then I shut them quick. I would never tell her how much hell I raised with my sister Sarah. I brought calm? I didn't feel very calm. I felt warm all over, as though I had a blush rising upon all of my skin. I cracked open one eye. She was still kneeling before me, but rested in another silent moment.

I wanted to say "Amen" and have done with it. I wanted to run away. But I stayed, and I waited for her to speak again.

She finally continued in a more usual vein, and at last she finished up and I could get to my feet and bid her goodnight.

She told me it was a comfort to have someone share her prayer time. I was glad the fire had died and she couldn't see my reddening face.

As I walked to my bed, I passed the Wilson's wagon and overheard the woman speaking to her husband from underneath the wagon box.

". . . him a Gentile-lover, and her man just laid to rest, too. It's a scandal, I say. You ought to speak to the Captain."

I stood pegged to the spot, shaking with the anger that rose in me, then I fled to my camp.

Chapter 19

I didn't eat so often with the widow after that night, meaning to spare her from the wicked tongue of Sister Wilson.

That made for a lonely time. Even after weeks on the trail, I had no friends among the families in our Ten. I looked back along the thread of my life and had to go quite a ways to dig out a time when I had made a friend. Paul Peters. He had befriended me when I attended meetings in that forlorn bar room back in Pennsylvania. That had been so long ago. Would I always be a friendless, solitary being? The thought cut as sharp as a knife blade.

One night as I laid my fire, Sister Porter came to my camp, carrying her son.

"Lije," she said right off. "Have I offended you? I can't get you to eat with us." She bent her head and kissed the child. "Joseph misses you."

The fact was, I missed playing with Joseph. I missed conversing with Joseph's mother. My heart had been a hollow cavern for weeks.

I got up from my task. "Sister Porter, I—"

She cut me off. "There's plenty in the kettle. I miss talking to you. Please come."

I weighed the problem of her need for friendly conversation against the gossip sure to be caused by my presence beside her wagon, and wondered if she knew about

Sister Wilson's vicious mouth.

"Please," she repeated. "No one but you will speak to me. I think they're afraid to hurt my feelings in case they accidentally mention Joshua."

The poison has spread, I thought. I tried to conceal my anger from her, not wanting her to guess the real reason behind the silence she experienced. I took a deep breath and made my choice, vowing that I would not leave her to suffer in a silent void even if Sister Wilson's wagging tongue spewed more gossip about us.

"I'll come to eat, but you must share my supplies from now on. I've eaten more than my portion of yours."

Her voice was soft as she answered. "You know I have plenty since—"

"I'll not eat up your goods," I replied, a trifle hotly. "You'll need the extra when you get to Zion, else you'll starve."

Then I wished to bite off my hasty tongue, because she cringed. My words must have brought to her mind the fact that she would have no man in Zion to fend for her.

"Etta, I'm sorry."

I stepped back a pace. I had called her by her Christian name, and it surprised me to do it.

She hugged Joseph tight and lifted her head. "I know you don't mean me harm. You're right to counsel me to caution. I have been trying to think of what I can do to earn my way when I reach the Valley. I fear my talents are few, and they suit me only to be a farmer's wife."

I stared at her, fighting down the impulse to take her into my arms and comfort her. I had called her "Etta."

A subtle, delicate sentiment began to grow within my chest. I hardly heard her words as I tried to stop the burgeoning bubble of tenderness by reminding myself that just weeks past, she had been another man's wife. I reminded myself that I had not thought to grow fond of a woman until I had built a home for a wife. Even so, the feeling kept expanding. I had no power to suppress it.

I had to say something, take some action to prevent me from making a fool of myself or of her. I stooped and picked up a stick. In a muffled voice I answered her. "I'll come to eat, but I'll bring the fire." That made hardly any sense, but I gathered up the fuel I had laid, hiding my face from her view. Then I preceded her to her camp.

The next day, before I yoked Etta's oxen, I stripped my mule's packs of the foodstuffs I had brought and distributed my personal belongings between the packs. I carried the supplies to the widow's wagon in three trips, and secured them inside. Then I got her oxen into the yokes and made sure she was set for the day.

On the way back to where I'd left my animals, I saw one woman whispering behind her hand to another, and I sidestepped out of their sight.

Let them talk, I thought. *I'm only doing as I promised.*

~ ~ ~ ~ ~

One morning, our division didn't get started at the usual time, as a woman in another Ten had died during the night. Due to my known grave digging skill, I was called upon to produce a place for her burial. I noticed that when we began the service, Etta picked up Joseph and walked far off onto the prairie. I didn't blame her for trying to keep bitter memories at bay.

We ended the brief funeral by singing the song, "All is well."

As the time approached for the wagons to depart, I went out into the brown grass to bring Etta back. When I located her, she stood very still, facing westward, her sunbonnet obscuring my sight of her face. Joseph lay quiet in her arms. Was she thinking of Joshua Porter?

A wave of jealousy rooted me to the spot. Where had that feeling come from? Despite the fondness that had increased in my bosom ever since the night she begged me to rejoin her evening routine, I had no claim. I knew I was no more to her than a helpful acquaintance.

And someone who calmed her spirits.

I could have no expectation of a permanent place in her life. Beyond calling me by my Christian name a time or two, telling me that her son missed my presence, and that she missed our conversations, she had not exhibited any sign of affection for me.

When I had stuffed away the unexpected and unwanted emotion, I moved toward her. I wasn't sure how to address her. I finally chose formality as the best course of action.

"Sister Porter, it's time to leave."

She turned toward me. "Does it comfort you that your mother lies in a regular graveyard, rather than on the prairie?"

I stared at the tips of my boots, not knowing how to answer her odd question. Out of the corner of my eye, I saw her wave back toward the grave alongside the trail.

"That poor woman. How many more will die before we reach Zion?"

I shook my head, still tongue-tied.

"I can't remember how his voice sounded."

Her voice was no more than a whisper, but her words assaulted my soul. I didn't want her thinking of him.

The silence built until I thought my ears had ceased to function. When I could stand no more of it, I blurted, "Nor I." No. I did not want to speak of him, so I added, "My mother, I mean."

It wasn't a lie. I no longer could recall the sound of her voice.

She nodded. "You didn't know him well. He was a good man, not given to violence like my . . ." She let her words drift into nothingness.

I couldn't speak.

Her words began again in a rush. "When he discovered how my father treated me, he took me away. We married. I gave birth to a son." She turned toward the west again and continued in a muffled voice. "Someone preached to us and told us about Zion. We accepted baptism." She stopped and began to rock the child.

I would have taken him, but my arms wouldn't move.

"Joshua said we must go to Zion and I agreed. I didn't know it would be so hard." She sniffed, and then looked in my direction. "Is it hard for you?"

"Yes." At last, my voice broke free. "Life is hard. That song. My father always said something similar. 'All will be well,' he'd tell us, even when we were starving."

Etta's face blanched, but she said nothing.

I didn't say anything more for a long moment, as the feeling that my father's words always brought enwrapped me, calmed me. "I don't think I could have gone on without that assurance. Like the song, 'all is well, all is well.'"

Joseph began to fuss. Etta bounced him gently. "Your faith is deep."

I wondered about that. Had I stopped relying on my father's faith and found my own? I wasn't sure, but my spate of jealousy had passed.

I heard a voice from the wagons calling us.

I put out my arms. "We must go. Let me carry the boy."

We walked toward the wagons, Joseph breathing softly against my shoulder. *A boy without a father. Like me.*

~ ~ ~ ~ ~

Several days later, the camp awoke to the boom of the cannon.

I got out of my bedroll, which I always put down a good distance from Etta's wagon. No need to provoke gossip.

Large animals covered the plains ahead of the wagons. *Buffalo!* I wished I had my old gun, but some two-legged varmint in Missouri had possession of it now. Then a man came down the chain of circled wagons to tell us that we would stay encamped for the day in order to bring in meat.

I wouldn't be hunting, with no firearm at hand. Or so I thought. When I went to breakfast with Etta and Joseph, I noticed a fine rifle propped up against the rear wagon wheel.

Etta grinned at me as she gestured toward the weapon with her head. "You could use some fun," she said, her eyes sparkling. "Are you a good hunter?"

"At least middling," I replied, my grin as wide as hers. I didn't know what had brought on her good humor, but her mood had infected me. I glanced down. A cartridge box lay beside the rifle butt. She must have some knowledge of what was required to fire the rifle.

"Good. We could use a haunch of meat. I hear buffalo is tasty."

"I wouldn't know." I chuckled, feeling my spirits rise higher. "I hope to find out later today."

Since the buffalo were nearby, I chose not to saddle my horse. I didn't know how it would react to the noise of gunfire, and didn't want to be obliged to chase it down if it spooked. Instead, I left it tethered and walked a quarter mile to join the other hunters from the fifty wagons who had gathered.

President Richards stood at the side of his wagon, greeting men he knew and shaking hands with anyone who came near. When it looked like everyone who was coming had assembled, he made a quieting motion with his hands, and the hubbub died down.

"There's a good many of you, I see," he said. "I won't abide the waste of meat, so elect a man from each Ten to be the huntsman, and another to back him up. The rest of you can help them choose an animal to stalk and bring down. If we get a dozen good buffalo, they will be sufficient for us to divide." He then had us separate by Tens to choose who would shoot.

I'd wanted to bring home a buffalo just for Etta, but that was not President Richards' plan, so I kept my grumbling to myself. Not sure where I stood with Captain Armstrong, I could not be certain I would be picked as one of the hunters from our Ten.

As soon as we got together in one spot, the captain elected himself as chief huntsman. Amidst the chorus of groans and other disappointed sounds, he said, "I'll take Eb Wilson as my second."

And so it was done. For the next three hours, two other men and I accompanied the two shooters as they disputed over which bull was the biggest, which would be most tender, and finally, which was closest and would take the least effort to shoot, butcher, and carry back to our wagons.

By the middle of the afternoon, I was drenched in sweat and well-adorned with fresh buffalo dung from being shoved to the ground for use as a rifle rest. Fortunately, I had the presence of mind to clap my hands over my ears so I wouldn't be deaf from the thunderous report of Captain Armstrong's big fifty caliber rifle.

I returned to Etta's wagon carrying over my shoulder a good fifty pounds of buffalo meat wrapped in a piece of wooly hide. Satisfied as I was with my take, I worried over where I would find enough water to remove the odorous attachments to my person. The river was at least two days' travel ahead, and the water in the barrel tied to the side of Etta's wagon was reserved for culinary purposes.

I needn't have worried.

Etta was so delighted with the addition to her larder that she simply directed me as to where to dump my load of meat. Then, when I removed and returned the rifle and cartridge case I had carried slung over the other shoulder, she got a whiff of me, laughed, and said, "Go roll in that tall grass, then use it to scrub off the rest of the—" She laughed again. "Thank you, sir. You're most valiant."

I went. I rolled. I scrubbed. A large portion of prairie grass fell prey to my cleansing efforts. The smell still clung to parts of my clothing, but at least I had success in removing the source. As I approached the wagon, such a lovely scent of frying meat filled the air that I decided it would mask my own contribution sufficiently that I could take supper with the cook.

~ ~ ~ ~ ~

After the hunt, I expected the buffalo to move away from the humans who had tormented them with loud noises and removed prime bulls from the herd. To my surprise, I was wrong. Word came down the line of wagons that since the animals had not moved off, there was no point in breaking camp tomorrow. Tonight, we were to make merry in celebration of the successful hunt, with a gathering near President Richards' wagon to sing and dance.

I walked beside Etta to the designated place, carrying her sleeping child in my arms. He didn't seem as conscious of the odor that still clung to my clothing as I was. I wondered if it bothered Etta. I could only judge my fitness for the party by her distance from me. As we walked along, I determined that if I were to reach out my arm, I could touch the top of her head, so she must not be overly annoyed by my presence.

Indeed, she chattered away in an excited voice, which meant that I had no need of filling in lulls in the conversation, as there were none. I was content to hear the animation in her words, and for the time being, forgot what other members of the Ten might say about us strolling along as though we were a family.

In fact, I began to imagine how it would be to have a wife and a son. I let my flight of fancy soar for a few moments, and then brought myself down to earth. The woman beside me was a widow. I was no more than a hired hand, a man who had offered her protection and assistance. I had no right to indulge myself in thoughts of replacing her husband and taking over the fathering of the boy I carried. Even if he had called me "Papa," it had been an infantile mistake; he'd only been trying out the word.

By the time we arrived at the dance circle, my mood had dropped to my toes. By contrast, Etta's eyes spoke of elation and delight in the anticipated party. I wondered if I should remove myself from the crowd in order that she could fully savor her joy, undiminished by my case of the dismals.

She didn't give me the chance to escape.

Once I laid Joseph down among a hoard of sleeping children, Etta grabbed my hands and insisted on me squiring her over to the merry-makers.

I intended to hand her off to any eligible male in sight, but she made that impossible by tightly gripping my fingers as we joined a circle of dancers. After a few stumbles, I remembered the figures of the dance, and carried on with surer steps.

Little by little, my mood lifted. Etta's sparkling eyes reminded me of other social occasions when my presence had been welcome. What helped, to no small extent, was my discovery—as I moved around the circle—that the other men smelled no better than I did, and their wives gave no indications of distaste.

At one point, Etta was flung into my arms by an over-enthusiastic partner in a reel, and the brilliant smile she lifted in my direction as we sorted ourselves out almost stopped my breathing.

Was it possible that Etta bore me affection?

As I began to breathe normally again, I determined to gain the answer to that question. It mattered a great deal. By all evidences, I had become enamored with the woman in my care.

Chapter 20

Later that week, the river appeared in the path of our westward progress. I stopped on a rise to gaze at the watery obstacle. Brush and a few trees grew on the banks of the river, but there was clear evidence of a ford that had been used earlier this season.

Remembering the fear Etta had expressed to me, I hurried toward her wagon. She had halted the oxen near the top of the bank, waiting her turn to enter the water while the second company of ten wagons crossed over.

I pulled up my animals alongside her, and looked down into her wide eyes.

"Oh Lije, I can't drive them over. My hands are shaking just to think about that current." Indeed. Her hands clasped around the ox goad quivered.

"I'm here," I answered, and took my foot from the stirrup. I swung down and led my horse and mules to the rear of the wagon, where I tied them to the tailgate. At her side again, I took the shaking goad from Etta's hands, and boosted her to the wagon seat. She loosed a small sigh. I glanced up to her tight face, grinned in hopes of lightening her mood, and saw that color was vanquishing her pallor. The corners of her mouth tried to respond to my grin, but her effort was what some folks might call wan.

"You set easy now. I'll get us safely across." I started to

go forward to the lead team, then returned and looked around for her son. "Where's Joseph?"

She gestured behind the seat. "He's asleep. I hope he'll nap through the crossing."

When our turn finally came, I urged the oxen into the water. Although they didn't favor getting wet, they had nothing against slaking their thirst, and part of the way across, one of the lead animals quit pulling and dipped his head into the stream.

This action surprised the other beasts, and their agitation at the unexpected stop caused the front of the wagon to tip forward a bit. It wasn't much, but Etta lost her hold on the seat, and fell into the river. She landed flat on her front, then rolled as the current caught her and carried her away from me.

~ ~ ~ ~ ~

I dropped the ox goad and plunged after her.

I'd gone swimming in our pond back home, but that placid water didn't grab at my arms as this rushing river did. I concentrated on reaching Etta, who was about ten yards out of my grasp. I heard the splashes she made as she struggled against the swift current, trying, even in her terror, to keep her head in the air.

The water tumbled her around and she went under. I was still too far away to grab her.

She's going to die. I'm going to lose her.

If I lost Etta, life would have no meaning. I would be an empty shell.

Then her head broke the water and I heard a strangled gurgle. I reached for her, but again she was gone, down, down into the turbulence.

I looked around. The water in the middle of the river appeared to move more rapidly than at the edges. If I could get into the swifter water, perhaps I could catch up to her.

I dove across the boiling waves and into the faster

current. The muddy water swirled and tugged me down. My sodden clothes and heavy boots dragged me deeper. I panicked, flailing in the bowels of the river. If I drowned, who would rescue Etta? Who would care for Joseph?

All will be well, Elijah.

I stopped struggling, listening for my father's voice in my head. *All will be well.*

I kicked my way to the surface and began to use long strokes of my arms. Etta surfaced, just an arm's length out of my reach. I was tiring, gasping to get breath, but I labored on and pulled closer to her.

Then I was alongside her and she grabbed me around the neck. We went under, and I knew we were doomed to drown. *Please, Heavenly Father. Don't let Sister Wilson take the child.*

~ ~ ~ ~ ~

All will be well. Kick boy, kick.

I kicked, then kicked again, and gasped as my head came up from the water. Etta still clung to my neck, struggling to surface.

I pulled her head free of the churning water by her hair, crying "Etta, turn me loose. I'll hold you."

She ceased to struggle and allowed me to grasp her about the waist.

I stroked over to the riverbank and dragged her up to the top of the rise. She retched, and I held her while she coughed and gagged and spit up the water she had swallowed.

My muscles shook as I held her, retching and choking and gasping for air. I'd never seen such a lovely sight than the soaked, bedraggled, living woman in my arms. When she could breathe once more, we both sank to the grass and lay in an exhausted heap.

A brother from the second Ten came up on horseback, leading my mount and another horse tied beside it. The man was followed by others running along the bank and clamoring to know if all was well with us.

I got to my feet, aided by the first man to reach us. I found my footing and balance, then pulled Etta to her feet amid cheers from up and down the river.

Seeing that we were alive, all but the man holding our horses drifted back to the ford and their work.

Etta raised her head. "Lije," she said, her voice so faint I could scarcely make out the word. "You rescued me. You saved my life. Thank you, thank you."

I didn't deserve her praise, but it sounded wonderful coming from her lips. I'd only gotten the strength to fight the river from my father, from his voice in my head. I didn't know if she would understand. I was sure she wouldn't understand the yearning that came over me with such power that I had to bite my lip.

Etta turned to the brother with the horses. "My baby. Is he safe?"

"Quite safe, Sister. We rescued your wagon, and the boy slept all the way across."

"Thank the Lord!"

"He's fussing a bit now, looking around for you."

"I'll be there directly," she said.

The man handed me the reins to my horse, touched the brim of his hat, and rode off to continue his work.

Etta turned to me. "I could not have wished for such a crossing, but you kept your word to get us safely to the other side."

I looked around. We *were* on the other side of the river. I chuckled. "It seems that I did." I shifted my weight, and water squished in my boot. What if I had lost her to the river?

I shook my head.

I took a deep breath. I almost *had* lost her. I had to include her in the immense relief that bubbled upward from my soggy boots.

"Et—Etta," I stammered as I realized the enormity of what I was about to say. "If I had my wish, you would never leave my side."

I stopped, appalled at my statement. I had no proof of her affection toward me, but I plunged on, compelled to share my feelings. "When you were out of my reach in the water, I knew that if you were to die, my life would be empty."

I paused for a shaky breath. "Etta, once you said you were fit only to be a farmer's wife. I'm a farmer. I'm a good farmer. I don't have any land now, but I hope to remedy that condition in Zion." I stopped and gulped and looked into her eyes. "When time has eased your sorrow, will you be my wife?"

I looked at her, holding fear in my hands along with my reins, knowing that her answer was the key to my future. Somewhere deep in my belly, all hope stood poised on the edge of a pinnacle, waiting for her reply.

Her blue eyes gazed into mine as she kept silence for a time. Then she spoke. "You, of all the members of the company, have worked to ease my grief. Now you have saved my life. You, you were a stranger, but you have become my dearest friend."

She stopped, suddenly self-conscious, and fussed the hair away from her face. Then she smoothed her sodden skirt.

I held my breath. Did women marry their friends? Was she working up her courage to reject me?

The horse bumped into me, nuzzled my face. I stroked its nose, then pushed it aside as gently as I could. I had to watch Etta. She still played with her skirt.

At last, she looked at me again. I couldn't read her expression, and my heart began to sink.

Then she spoke. "I will wed you whenever you say, my Lije." She smiled, and the mud on her face only made her seem a rare flower of great beauty blooming from the prairie.

She made a little movement with her hands, as though she wanted to embrace me, but was constrained by propriety.

I had no such qualms. I let go of the reins, gathered Etta into my arms, and clasped her against my heart. That was fitting. It belonged to her.

She sighed, tucking herself against my chest.

I wanted to kiss her lips, but did not. That could wait for a more private moment.

I don't know how long I held Etta in my arms. It seemed to last a brief time and it seemed to last for eternity. After a while, I let her go.

Fortunately, the horses had not moved away, and I helped her mount. Then I stepped into my saddle, heart pulsing hard in my throat, feeling the spread of joy I knew as belonging. I remembered a scripture fit for the situation. *We are no more strangers.* I turned my horse and grinned at Etta.

"Let's go see Joseph. Tell him he can soon call me 'papa'."

Chapter 21

I sat beside Etta's fire, wrapped in a blanket while my clothing dried near the flames. I owned a change of clothes, but Etta insisted that I could not go a step beyond her wagon without getting warm and dry, and because that meant getting out of my soggy apparel, I took the blanket she handed me and sought out a leafy shelter near the river to do her bidding. I grinned. In point of fact, I *had* gone beyond her wagon, but I was not going to bring that up.

Etta, who unlike me, had a wagon in which to make a change, now wore a different dress and stirred up a batch of biscuits to go with the buffalo steaks spitting grease in the skillet. Joseph sat on a blanket, encircled with crates and boxes to keep him contained.

I raked my fingers through my hair. My hat was gone, floating down the river to St. Louis, I supposed. Or it could snag on the riverbank a mile below us. I wasn't going to chase it down.

"Mama," Joseph called out.

"You're fine, son." She looked my way. "Are you warm enough?"

"Yes, ma—Etta."

"Good." She spooned dough into a Dutch oven. "It was a convenience," she said, then patted at the dough with the back of her spoon.

"For me to sit here drying out?"

"No." She said nothing more for a long time, gazing out at the prairie. After a while she gave herself a little shake and murmured, "My marriage to Joshua."

"Oh." I didn't know what more to say. Was she telling me there had been no affection between them? "You eloped."

"I escaped. Joshua made it possible."

She put the cover on the oven and hefted it toward the fire. I almost got up to help her, then remembered my state of undress and remained where I was. She raked coals from the fire and put them on the lid.

"Why would he do that?"

"He was a friend to my brother. When David drowned, Joshua stepped into his place."

"Into his place?"

"As protector. My father had a vicious temper." She picked at the dough remaining on the spoon and threw it into the flames.

I coughed. She had said something before about her father.

"Joshua said we must run away, so we did."

"And you married him."

"He said it was best." She sat in silence, picking at the spoon.

"Was he good to you?"

"Yes." She inhaled, then sighed. "He gave me a son."

I wasn't sure why she was unburdening herself to me while I sat there, feeling particularly vulnerable in my naked state. Was she clearing the air, sharing her darkest secrets so there would be no impediment between us when we began a life together? I had not mentioned Mary Eliza to her. This seemed as good a time as any.

"I have a sister in Zion. I must find her when I get there."

She looked up. "Older or younger than you?"

"She's younger." I counted on my fingers. "Eight, I think.

April fifth was her birthday. Yes, eight."

"She's all alone?"

"No." I gave her the account of my arrangements for Mary Eliza and my journey into Missouri after the deaths of my family members.

She said, "Oh, Lije." Nothing more.

A man and woman walked by the fire.

Etta finally spoke. "We will seek her together."

"You're willing to do that for me?"

"You saved my life. You're taking my fatherless son as your own." She paused, looking into my eyes with such a direct gaze that I imagined I could see to the farthest extent of her soul. "You love me. Can I do less for your sister?"

I quaked at the depth of emotion I read in Etta's eyes. She loved me in return. "You're a wonder," I said, my voice trembling from the effect of my shaky breath. I was unwilling to break off the gaze, but after several seconds, she smiled and dipped her head.

I inhaled, and the odor of crisping wool filled my nose. I looked toward the fire and realized my clothes had begun to smoke. I clutched the blanket securely around me and got to my feet. "Don't go anywhere."

Etta looked quizzically at me.

"Just stay here." I gathered my dried clothing and went back to the leafy seclusion by the river to put them on. When I returned, Etta had the buffalo steaks and the biscuits off the fire. Two tin plates sat near the ironware.

My stomach growled, which should have embarrassed me, but being properly clad gave me enough confidence that I ignored the sound.

"You're just in time," she said, and lifted a steak onto a plate.

I went to the back of the wagon. "I don't want Captain Armstrong to marry us," I said, laying the folded blanket inside the wagon.

She nodded.

I returned to my seat by the fire. "I'll ask President Richards if he will honor us by blessing our marriage."

"Yes," she said. "When?"

"Whenever you wish. On the next Sabbath, if that pleases you."

She tried to hide a blush, but nodded after a moment. "It pleases me," she whispered.

My innards melted at her blush, her answer, the implication that she would marry me because she desired to be my wife, and not merely to have a protector. I took the plate she offered me, and attacked my meal with vigor so she couldn't guess how thoroughly her words affected me.

~ ~ ~ ~ ~

The next day, I sought an audience with President Richards. I hoped he would perform our marriage without any fuss. I didn't want to explain my aversion to having the job done by Captain Armstrong, although he had direct charge over us. I didn't like the man enough to let him perform such a precious act for us.

Besides, the captain might refuse.

I worried that President Richards was too busy to see me, or would send me away because I was just a hired driver in the party and not a married man. Instead, he allowed me to speak with him.

"What can I do for you?" he asked, gazing up from his seat.

I wasn't sure what to say for a moment, but feeling his eyes on me, I thought I'd best say something, anything.

I gulped and began. "Sir, I have proposed marriage to a woman in my Ten. We would like to marry as soon as possible. Will you do us the honor of performing the service?"

He crossed his arms, then raised a hand and tapped one finger against his chin. "You'd better sit," he said, indicating a nearby wooden crate.

I sat.

"Would that be the Widow Porter?"

I almost lost my composure. "You know her?"

President Richards smiled. "I'm aware of her situation." He leaned forward, holding my attention. "I also saw you together at the dance party." He leaned back and rested his clasped hands upon his waistcoat. "I would be a poor shepherd if I didn't know my flock."

"Yes, sir." What did he know about me?

"Do you have affection for this woman, or is this marriage merely an act of compassion?"

"Oh, sir—"

He cut me off. "Ah. I see."

I didn't know what more to say. Had I botched my chance?

He leaned forward again. "What will you do about the boy?"

"Joseph? I will raise him as my own."

"Good. That is good." Once more, he tapped his chin with his forefinger. "What priesthood do you hold?"

I remembered the certificate buried deep in my belongings that had survived my expedition to Missouri because it was in my pocket. "The priesthood of Aaron," I said. "I was ordained a Teacher in Pennsylvania by the branch president."

"Some time ago, then?"

"Yes, sir. It's been a long time."

He looked into my eyes for several more minutes. President Peters had done the same. I wondered if they shared the ability to read my soul.

"Hmm," he said at last. "Let's rectify the situation." He looked away and beckoned to a man who had been sitting a short distance off, doing something with a piece of buffalo hide. "Brother Ezra. Come over here, if you will."

Before I hardly knew what was happening, I had two

pairs of hands resting atop my head. President Richards called upon God, and then spoke the words that conferred upon me the same priesthood that my father had possessed, and then gave me the office of elder.

As he handed me a certificate to verify my new standing, President Richards said, "About your wedding. Will the Sabbath be soon enough?"

"Yes, sir. That will suit us very well. Thank you, sir."

He beamed.

I turned and ran back to the wagon to tell Etta.

~ ~ ~ ~ ~

The Sabbath came at last.

I stood before President Richards with Etta at my side. She wore her best dress, overlaid with a crisp white apron. I wore Joshua Porter's snug coat and trousers. I did not want to marry the man's widow wearing his clothing, but my bride insisted that I had to look as presentable as possible for the ceremony. With no friend from which to borrow a suit or any other remedy, I acquiesced to her wishes, and hoped no one would notice how far the coat sleeves rode up on my wrists.

Today should be the high point of my life. Instead, my body shook in anticipation of the marriage rite. Etta had done this before. I had not. Etta had already been a wife. I had not been a husband. Would she find me wanting?

President Richards began the ceremony, flanked by two brothers from his Ten as witnesses. One I knew to be the clerk of the camp. I did not know the other. As long as Captain Armstrong didn't show up to create a stir, it didn't matter to me who he might be.

Behind us stood a couple Etta knew from another Ten, Clara and Warren Brown. Sister Brown held Joseph. I could hear him talking his baby language to her. She responded with "Shh, hush, little one, there now, quiet," in a whisper.

The president spoke of overcoming trials together, of praying together and being faithful to the vows we would make. Etta's hand stole into mine and pressed it gently. I inhaled and tried to concentrate on the service.

Then President Richards joined our right hands and called upon Etta to repeat those vows after him. My turn came. I feared my voice would not come out, but after clearing my throat a time or two, it did issue forth and repeat the words of the president. Behind me, Joseph patted his soft palms together. The sound steadied me at last, and when the president called for a ring, I was ready.

Etta had removed Joshua's thin gold band from her finger several weeks before, and offered it to me the night previous, but I refused to reuse it. Instead, I had woven a band from thin blades of grass I plucked from the plains. It wouldn't last, but it was a promise of a more substantial ring to come. I slipped it onto my bride's finger.

Words, and more words, and finally the ones that mattered, the ones calling us "man and wife." I couldn't take my eyes off Etta's glowing face.

"Would you like to touch off the cannon?" President Richards asked me.

I think he asked me twice before I realized what he had said. "But it's the Sabbath," I protested.

"And this is a grand occasion." He took me by the arm and directed us to a portable desk upon which lay a piece of paper. "But first, we'll all sign your marriage certificate."

He and the witnesses affixed their signatures, and Etta and I each printed our names on the specified lines. He advised her to use only her birth name, by which I learned that her maiden name was Henrietta Elizabeth Rogers. She looked at mine—Elijah Alexander Marshall—with a little smile on her lips.

When President Richards folded the paper and gave it to Etta, she stowed it in her apron pocket and took her son from Sister Brown. I was led away to fire the camp cannon in celebration of our great event.

I looked over my shoulder. Etta held her hands over Joseph's ears. I grinned at her, and pulled the lanyard.

The *boom* brought members of the company running to learn the cause of alarm. Upon learning the reason, many pressed upon us their hearty congratulations. Captain Armstrong seemed startled, but shook my hand with as good a grace as he could muster.

When the furor had died down, I took Etta's hand in mine, and carrying Joseph in my other arm, walked back to the wagon that, with a few words of blessing, had become mine. Ours. I was now a family man.

Chapter 22

After Etta showed our marriage certificate to the doubters and gossips in our Ten, I merged most of my bedroll with hers. Sister Wilson's "humph" was telling of her displeasure. By entering into a union sanctified by the leader of our camp, we had ruined her opportunity to continue being ungracious. I would have laughed at her reaction had not Etta's elbow found my ribs. Despite our short length of time in knowing each other, my bride anticipated my sometimes inappropriate humor.

When the lamps in our Ten had flickered out, I scooped up our sleeping son and a pair of blankets and, mindful of pricked ears, led Etta to a copse of willows a quarter-mile distant from the camp. There we made our marriage bed, shared our first kiss, and became man and wife in fact under a sky brilliant with stars.

The company continued west.

After several more weeks travel, we arrived at Fort John, an establishment that would be known later as Fort Laramie, but when we reached it, the former name still held sway.

By now, the grass band I'd fashioned to make Etta's wedding ring had dried to a brittle circle, barely holding together, and she'd removed it to tuck into a small box where she kept mementoes. The nakedness of her finger bothered me, but I had an idea. By subterfuge, I determined that my small finger above the final joint and Etta's ring finger at the base were about the same diameter, so once our business at the fort's store was concluded, I slipped away to the blacksmith's shop.

"Do you make rings?" I inquired of the blacksmith.

"Rings?" The man scratched his head above one ear as he took thought. "Do you mean finger rings?"

"Yes. I need a wedding ring." I didn't tell him I had made an insubstantial ring that needed to be replaced. I was pretty sure he would find amusement in the notion at my expense, and I didn't want anything to spoil my idea.

"Getting married, are you?" He laughed. "You're from the Mormon lot, yes? Does the first missus know you've picked out another wife?"

I didn't allow myself to get angry. I said, "There's only one missus, and she needs a ring."

"Ah," he said, grinning. "You were married along the way. Well, I don't have any gold or silver, if that's what you're seeking."

I had dared hope he did have a precious metal, and my heart flopped into my gut.

"But look here. I can make a pretty enough circle with a horseshoeing nail."

A nail? I started to shake my head, then the thought struck me that if I were to see a ring on my bride's finger today, I had better take the blacksmith's offer.

So instead I nodded, and I said, "That will do until I can afford a gold ring."

"Do you have a measurement? A bit of string or a paper of a length cut to her finger size?"

I held up my hand. "It's the size of my finger, right here," and showed him the proper place on the small finger of my left hand.

"Huh," he grunted, matched my finger to a spot on a bit of rod that tapered from large to small, and dug around in a bin.

He pulled out a length of metal that had the rough form of a nail. "Stand back," he advised me, and I did so.

He used a bellows to heat up the fire in his forge, laid the nail in the hottest part, and stood back himself, arms crossed against his chest, waiting. At one point he again used the bellows, and I watched as he pumped air beneath the fire until the nail glowed red-hot. Then he removed the metal with a pair of tongs, laid it on his anvil, and took up a hammer.

The process of changing a nail into a ring fascinated me. The blacksmith deftly turned the metal as he beat it flat, shaped it, stretched it, and formed it into a circle. I was obliged to cover my ears against the ring of the hammer on the nail then the anvil as he found a steady rhythm. He paused once to reheat the ring, and beat upon it more gently after he sized it with the rod.

When he had finished the work, and was satisfied with his craftsmanship, he put down his tools, picked up the still-hot ring with tongs, and thrust it into a small barrel of water.

Such a smoke as arose from the water! The hot ring sputtered as it cooled, and then the blacksmith brought it up and laid it on the anvil once more.

He searched around the shop until he found the tool he wanted, and held up a fine wire brush. "I'll give it a nice finish," he said, and brushed the ring until it gleamed. Then he laid it in my hand.

"There, now. What do you think?"

The ring in my hand still resembled a shoeing nail, but the brushwork had taken off the carbon black from the fire and left a subtle sheen behind.

"It will do. It surely will do," I said, and paid him with my last store of money.

When I slipped the ring onto Etta's finger that night, she sucked in her breath. "Where did you get this?"

"I had it made at the fort."

She took my face in her hands and kissed me soundly, by which I knew my offering was acceptable.

~ ~ ~ ~ ~

To our delight, beyond Fort John we found Saints from the prior year's pioneers manning a raft ferry at a river crossing. The next fifty miles made me wonder if any of us would live to see Zion, as we encountered bad water, swamps, little grass for our animals, bad campsites, a steep hill, and several stretches of alkali flats. Nevertheless, the company pressed on, and a few days later, I climbed Independence Rock and carved my initials into the surface.

Devil's Gate was our next resting place. Soon thereafter, the camp reached South Pass, a flat, grass-covered rise I thought very unlike the mountain passes of my native state. Captain Armstrong informed us that beyond the pass, water flowed toward the Pacific Ocean.

When we came to the Green River, the men built several rafts for the crossing, much to my wife's relief. Three days later, the company halted at a ramshackle establishment made of adobe blocks.

Etta spoke to a woman at Jim Bridger's fort and learned that we neared the end of our journey.

"Two weeks more of travel, Lije. That's all we lack of being in Zion."

I put my hands on my wife's shoulders and gazed into her eyes. "As close by as that, huh?" I fought down the inclination to chuckle, fearing she would think I was making fun of her.

"She said it would take us three weeks at the most."

The sparkle in her eyes took away my breath. I nodded. "Imagine," I said with a gruffness in my voice. "Two or three weeks."

~ ~ ~ ~ ~

Climbing into the mountains proved challenging. I had never seen such tall peaks and narrow valleys. The company was obliged to pass down and through defiles and up the other side of mountains that might intimidate the bravest of men, until we caught sight of an immense flat area stretching ahead as far as the eye could see. Was it possible that this arid plain, our new home, was at last within our reach?

Etta clasped her hands together and gazed over them at the basin ahead. "Now we will find Mary Eliza," she said. I could have wept at her goodness.

I worked with the other men in our Ten to lock the rear wheels of our wagons with chains, and attach log drags behind so we could slide the vehicles down the trail on the side of the large mountain. This raised plenty of dust into the air. Once we reached the flat, we had to make the ascent of a smaller mountain beyond.

Our camp that night was our last on the trail, in a canyon leading to the Valley beyond.

Before I extinguished our lamps for the night, I stood with my wife under the trees, looking at the final leg of the trail.

"Do you think she'll recognize me?"

Etta removed Joshua's hat from my head, swept my forelock back, gave me a kiss, and replaced the hat. "She can't have forgotten you."

"Will she forgive me?"

Etta took my hand. "What would your father say?"

"'All will be well,'" I whispered, due to the lump that threatened to close my throat.

The next morning, the company began the final miles of descent to the plain. I took advantage of a pause to survey the features of the valley that promised so much. To the north, a small peak rose. Beyond it, a great body of water shimmered in the sunlight. That had to be the Great Salt Lake of which I had heard so much. Below it, harvested fields lay beside a creek. Close by those fields, I saw a bowery. Was that the meeting place until the Saints could construct buildings for worship?

Off to the south, a rough adobe wall encompassed a large area that I took to be a fort. Beyond, other fields stretched to cover hundreds of acres. They, too, had been harvested. Far to the west, other mountains poked jaggedly upward. Southward, another hill circled around much like a fence. Behind us, the ridges our division had traversed stood as a barrier to the world.

I returned my gaze to the walled-off area. My sister must be in that fort. My stomach clenched. Much time had passed. Would I know *her*?

~ ~ ~ ~ ~

The fort loomed large before us. Our Ten would reach it within the next half hour. Fortunately, Etta rode in the wagon, nursing Joseph, so she could not see how I quaked as I walked beside the oxen.

Ma had laid a duty upon me concerning my sister. I had failed to see it through. Others had nurtured her and brought her to Zion. Were my parents looking down from heaven, frowning at my failures? Did God know of my faults and imperfections? Of course He did. How could it be otherwise? I trudged along, chastising myself until my spirits sunk low and I could barely call myself a man.

Our wagons traveled two abreast down a well-traveled road. Captain Armstrong rode up on his horse, coming between my wagon and the one to my left.

"Marshall," he said. "I didn't imagine you'd marry the woman."

"God helps us keep our promises," I muttered. Where had I got that thought? Was I lying? I hadn't kept my promise to my mother.

The captain frowned, then spurred forward, spurting dust into my face.

Maybe I deserved that.

Ahead of me, the wagons drifted to a halt, and I yelled a command to my oxen. "Ho! Pull up there." The oxen stopped.

My wagon slowly rolled forward a foot, then settled to a stop.

Etta opened the wagon sheet and climbed down. She slipped her hand into the crook of my arm. After a moment, she asked, "What troubles you?"

I clicked the toe of one shoe against the other in an attempt to knock off the dust. I repeated the action with the opposite shoe. Etta squeezed my arm. I finally said, "I failed my sister."

"You did not. You made every possible provision for her. How could you know you would be delayed in returning?"

"I should have had more sense than to go into Missouri."

"Elijah! You did your best."

I had never heard my wife speak so sharply. She had such confidence, such trust in me. *She loves me.* My spirits began to lift. "Did I?"

She turned and looked me in the eye. "Husband, you did. God cannot fault you for the actions of ruffians."

I had to believe her. She believed in me.

"God put the Ansons in your way to help you keep your promise."

I stared at her. *God helps us keep our promises.* I had said that, only moments ago.

I shifted my shoulders. The fort gate yawned open before us. People pressed forward.

I inhaled. "Let's go find my sister."

~ ~ ~ ~ ~

Etta got Joseph from the wagon, and smiled as she walked to my side. "All will be well," she mouthed.

I took her hand, and we walked through the gates of the fort.

Sod-topped cabins stood against the walls of the enclosure. A group of children played games over on one side. I tried to remember how Mary Eliza looked when I left her. She must have grown taller, perhaps lost her pudgy appearance. Which of the girls was my sister?

As the children noticed our arrival, they turned and stared at us. One girl bit her forefinger. I swallowed. She had the look of a young Sarah. I couldn't make my feet moved forward.

Etta looked at me, then followed my gaze. "Is that her?"

"I don't know. I think it may be."

"Let's ask her." She tugged me forward.

The little girl hadn't moved. Her hair floated about her face in disarray.

I took two steps. Three. Four, then came to a halt. "Pumpkin?"

Etta dropped my hand as the girl let out a shriek and launched herself at me. "Lije! I knew you'd come!"

I lifted her from the ground, snuggling her into my embrace. "Pumpkin," I muttered into her disheveled hair.

"I'm too old for that name," she said against my chest.

It was true. She no longer resembled the round vegetable.

She turned in my arms, putting an elbow into my ribs as she struggled to look at Etta. "Who is she?" she whispered.

"This is your new mother, my wife."

"Are you my father now?"

I considered that. "Not exactly, but I will act for Pa. Etta will act for Ma." I motioned to Joseph. "He will be your brother."

"What's his name?"

"Joseph. You will be his big sister."

"I like that," she said, and sighed. "I thought you might be dead, like Papa. Sister Anson said I must have hope and pray every night for you."

"And did you do that?"

She nodded. "I grew lots of hope. Sister Anson helped me pray."

"She was good to you."

"She learned me a lot."

I smiled. "Where is she? We need to let her know I'm here, and to thank her."

Mary Eliza pointed to a cabin in the far wall. I gathered my family and walked in that direction. The door opened before we arrived, and Sister Anson peered out.

"Brother Marshall," she said in a hushed voice. "You *are* alive."

"I was delayed. Circumstances opposed me," I offered. "I thank you for taking good care of my sister."

She shook her head. "It was no bother."

"I will repay your kindness. Somehow."

"There is no need. She is a good child." She put out her hand and patted Mary Eliza's arm.

"We had crickets," Mary Eliza said.

"Crickets?"

"They ate our crops, but then the birds came and ate them all up."

"Seagulls from the lake," Sister Anson prompted.

"Seagulls." Mary Eliza dipped her head and burrowed into my shoulder. "I'm glad you're home," she added, her voice muffled.

"Home." I said. I looked at Etta. "We'd best get situated."

"All will be well," she said, and grinned.

I gripped her hand. It would be so.

The End

Thank you for reading!

Please post a review of this book on your favorite review or purchase site. Reviews from readers, even as few as twenty words, make all the difference to those browsing and buying. Remember to recommend this book to your friends, telling them what you liked about it. Word-of-mouth recommendations are valuable rewards for authors. Finally, subscribe to Marsha's Readers Mailing list to receive advance notice of coming book releases.
http://eepurl.com/vBKEj

Other Books by Marsha Ward

Gone for a Soldier

The Man from Shenandoah

Ride to Raton

Trail of Storms

Spinster's Folly

Book List and Purchase Links:
http://marshaward.blogspot.com/p/books.html

About the Author

Amazon best-selling author Marsha Ward writes authentic historical fiction set in 19th Century America, and contemporary romance. She was born in the sleepy little town of Phoenix, Arizona, in a simpler time. With plenty of room to roam among the chickens and citrus trees, Marsha enjoyed playing with neighborhood chums, but always had her imaginary friend, cowboy Johnny Rigger Prescott, at her side. Now she makes her home in a forest in the mountains of Arizona. She loves to hear from her readers.

Connect with her at:
Website: http://marshaward.com
Blog: http://marshaward.blogspot.com
Email: authormarshaward@gmail.com
Facebook: https://www.facebook.com/authormarshaward
Twitter: http://twitter.com/MarshaWard
Join Marsha's mailing list to be notified of new releases:
http://eepurl.com/vBKEj

www.ingramcontent.com/pod-product-compliance
Lightning Source LLC
Chambersburg PA
CBHW020618180626
46810CB00007B/2825